THE FRENCH BILLIONAIRE

A CLEAN, INTERNATIONAL BILLIONAIRE CLUB ROMANCE

BRITNEY M MILLS

CRYSTAL CANYON PRESS

To Sandra Paquet

For your kind words and taking the time to read over this so my French characters sound and act French.

CHAPTER 1

Checking her calendar for the day, Juliette Rousseau was grateful for the lighter load. With a meeting scheduled this morning and another for the afternoon, she could finally get out and check several items off her list.

As the owner of Rousseau Belle, a skin care company based in Paris, France, she was constantly in search of new materials to work into her creams and lotions. She employed several people in research as well as production, but having the freedom to pick materials up herself was a rarity these days.

Her assistant, Rachelle, walked into her office with a slight grin on her face. "Your meeting is here a bit early. Do you want me to show her in?"

"Sure, then I can get to the market sooner."

"Okay, I'll let her know." Rachelle walked out of the room and back down the hallway, leaving Juliette in silence once again.

Clicking on the event in her online calendar, Juliette tried to refresh her memory of what it was about. Delacroix Marketing. Ugh.

Just another sales pitch she'd have to turn down, and not just once, but several times as they tried to sweeten the deal to get her business. She was still amazed that she'd been able to create this company after starting from mixing the creams in her parents' home in Dinan. The fact that she now had companies vying for her business was mind-boggling.

Nearly a minute later, a woman walked in, her hand outstretched even before she'd made it all the way through the door.

"Good morning, Madame Rousseau. Thank you for meeting with me. I'm Rose Boucher." She leaned over the desk, and Juliette stood, shaking her hand.

"It's nice to meet you, Madame Boucher. Please have a seat there." Juliette pointed to the chair in front of her desk and then took her own seat, scooting in and waiting for the pitch.

The woman smiled at her, a few age lines around her eyes. The Rousseau Belle aloe cream would be best to combat that. Juliette shook her head, trying to focus on what the woman was saying. Occupational hazard.

"As I told your assistant, I represent the Delacroix Marketing Agency, and we are interested in working with you on your marketing campaigns. It's been proven that advertising with our company and in the right areas can increase revenue by over forty percent."

Juliette raised an eyebrow. "Forty percent? What clients do you currently have?"

Rose rattled off several names, and Juliette nodded.

"So, when you're advertising to men, with sports, beer, and apparel, your companies have seen that significant of an increase. What experience does your company have in the beauty industry? What numbers can I compare to what we're already doing now?"

Rose's mouth opened and then closed, a bewildered look on her face. "Honestly, you would be our first beauty company." She paused a moment, as if regrouping, and then sat forward, placing a folder on Juliette's desk. "These are the terms my boss has agreed to offer you when you come on board with us."

Opening the folder, Juliette glanced at the numbers, not impressed by them. She stared at Rose for several seconds before asking, "May I ask who your boss is?"

"Tristan Delacroix."

The guy with his face plastered on billboards and flyers throughout the city. Lifting the folder, she handed it back to Rose, who stared at it as if this had never happened to her before. "I appreciate you coming here and giving me the information, but I hired someone to work on marketing only a few months ago, and we're doing quite well when it comes to sales."

Rose took the folder. "I've pitched to several beauty companies recently, as that market is Tristan's main focus right now. Do you mind me asking what would entice you to hire a marketing company?"

Juliette sat back in her chair, seeing the woman in a new light. She wasn't just a minion sent out to land contracts; she was looking for a way to improve. After years of working and studying and reading everything she could on building a business, Juliette knew what it was like to hit a brick wall and have to ask for feedback to get past it.

Smiling at the woman, she said, "Honestly, some actual ideas of how you would market to our company. What would you do differently from what we do now? I'm sure there was a lot of work put into the information in that folder, but it all appeals to males. With skin care, we're focused on women, meaning what works for men has a higher chance of flopping with women. Information on studies you've researched from what other companies have done. Any of that would help me give it more thought."

Rose stood and nodded. "I appreciate that. I've tried to tell my boss that we need a different approach, but I like my job, and I don't want to lose it if I push the issue."

Juliette threw back her head and laughed. "What? He won't listen to you about a woman's industry when you're a woman? That doesn't surprise me."

"Do you know Mr. Delacroix?"

Shaking her head, Juliette said, "No, but when I can't turn without seeing his face plastered onto something, I know he's probably thinking he owns the world and nothing should change."

Rose grinned, nodding. "You're more right about that than I want to admit. Thank you for your time."

Juliette waited a few minutes before taking her purse out of her desk and heading out. "I'll be back in a few hours, Rachelle. I have my phone, so notify me if any emergencies happen."

Rachelle nodded. "I'll do that."

Walking out the doors, she turned to the left and walked toward the nearest subway entrance. As she descended the stairs, a billboard hung above. A picture of a man with dark brown hair, strong cheekbones, and a five o'clock shadow stared back at her.

Tristan Delacroix. Case in point. She really couldn't go anywhere without his face staring.

Blowing out a breath, she let the frustration go, grateful she wouldn't have to meet him, let alone work with him anytime soon.

CHAPTER 2

Tristan Delacroix cut into his tartelette, relishing the flavors of the custard and raspberry combination. It had been a long day at the marketing agency he owned in Paris, and he'd needed to get out of the office for a bit. Éclair du Gâteau made the best pastries, and he'd decided to stop there after lunch.

He thought about the four large marketing campaigns waiting for his approval back at the office, and while his employees had made significant strides in correcting the problems from the first set of ideas, they still needed some work to give it the Delacroix stamp of approval.

A throat cleared close to him, and he looked up to see his secretary standing next to him at the table.

"I thought I'd find you here," Angela said with a smirk as she sat across from him. She'd been with his father's company since Tristan was just a young boy. When his father handed over the CEO title to him four years ago, there was no way he was getting rid of her. She knew way more about this business than many people half her age, and she wasn't prone to sucking up, which he appreciated.

"I needed a few minutes alone. Besides, sugar always helps me think through a problem. How did you know to look for me here?" He scooped the last bite of tartelette onto his fork and chewed it as he waited for her answer.

"Did you really just ask me that? This is my first place to go when I'm looking for you." She grinned at him, and he rolled his eyes, feeling more like a kid than a thirty-one-year-old adult. "We've got to get some things sorted before your meeting this afternoon, and George at the golf course wasn't happy about the terms you set for his contract."

Tristan groaned. He thought he'd already put out that fire, but it seemed he couldn't escape the whisper of problems that followed him wherever he went these days. "Of course he wasn't. That's only the third rewrite. We might not make our deadline if he keeps on at this rate." Taking a drink of his seltzer water, he asked, "Has Rose come back from meeting with the skin care company, Rosseau Belle?"

The tight smile Angela gave him didn't do anything to calm the waves of issues hitting him today. "Rose met with the owner this morning, but Juliette Rousseau turned her down."

"Turned her down? With the terms we're offering her? That's ridiculous. We're willing to give more in this package than we've offered any of our regular clients. What is it with these beauty companies that we just don't understand? We're trying to help them market their products, not take away their livelihood."

Angela shrugged, looking disengaged. "If you look at our resume, we're geared to advertise to men. Sports, tech. Sure, there are women in those areas, but for the most part, we don't know much about advertising to women. Did you tell Rose to change the pitch from how we normally do it?"

Tristan thought that over, feeling the truth of her words hit him in the gut. "No. I just told her to get the contract. We've pitched to ten beauty companies in the last few weeks, and neither you nor Rose said we needed to change anything."

"How do you think you would've reacted to the idea of changing what you think has worked its magic every time?"

Grinding his teeth, he felt as if he were getting scolded for not listening to his mother. "I probably would've laughed and said to try again."

"Exactly. So don't blame Rose for doing what you instructed her to do." The woman gave him a knowing look, her face serious, and the reprimand stung.

"She can think for herself. I wish some of these people would do what I hired them to do. Right now, I feel like I just babysit."

Angela threw back her head and laughed. "That's funny."

Frowning, Tristan asked, "What's so funny? I'm always having to check in to make sure things are done correctly."

"Which is also micromanaging. Step back and give them some space to work."

Again, the breath went out of him, and he closed his eyes for a moment, replaying the day's events. One by one, all of the situations fell into line with what she was saying. He shook his head and said, "Fine. You might be right about that. But just a little bit."

She smirked at him again, one eyebrow raised as she shook her head. "Just a piece of advice to help lighten your load. The company is triple the size it was before your father's heart attack, and I don't want to be sending you to the hospital in an ambulance this early."

"I know, Angela. I'll figure it out. But for now, did the owner of Rousseau Belle say anything as to why she rejected our generous offer?"

"Rose only said something about them doing quite well without marketing."

Tristan scoffed, pushing around some of the cream left on his plate. "Small businesses can only live on referrals for so long. We could take them to the next level and even higher, if they'd only give us that chance."

"Come up with a new pitch, one that will get the owner interested, for starters. Sometimes you've got to use your brain more than your good looks, Tristan." She grinned at him and stood. "Your mother called an hour ago. She said you haven't been picking up her calls for the past few days." She set her hand on her hip, the sign that she was waiting for a good answer.

"I'll call her. Just add it to my to-do list today."

Standing, Tristan left some money on the table and walked out the door, following Angela. What he wouldn't give for a few more minutes of peace before he had to walk back into the hailstorm.

CHAPTER 3

Getting off a conference call with one of their clients from the States, Angela's words continued to play a loop through Tristan's mind. He knew she was right, but it was too easy to just continue doing what he'd done for the past four years. He'd been able to grow his father's marketing firm to billion-dollar status by taking on clients in sporting goods, men's sportswear, and several tech companies around the world. Several clients came to them from other areas, but the one thing the Delacroix Marketing Agency lacked was experience in the beauty industry.

With the beauty industry's annual sales at jaw-dropping numbers from cosmetics to fashion, he knew his company needed to find a way to break into that market. But at every turn, he was shut down because of the lack of experience his company had in selling to women. They'd started contacting the larger cosmetic companies in Paris and had moved on to some of the smaller up-and-coming companies in the hopes that by making those businesses a household name, Tristan's company would have credibility moving forward.

"I'm heading out again," he called to Angela on his way past her desk.

"What do you mean? It's only three in the afternoon. You never

9

leave this early." She narrowed her eyes and pursed her lips, zeroing in on his face.

He chuckled as he walked toward the elevator. "I didn't say I was done with work. I just said I'm leaving."

A wide grin reached her face as Tristan turned around in the elevator. "You're going to Rousseau Belle, aren't you?"

He only had time to nod before the elevator doors closed and he started his descent to the ground floor. Getting out, he pulled up the address for the Rousseau Belle company, deciding to take the Métro, or subway. While he'd needed time to himself earlier in the day, he knew that being around people would spark his creative juices as far as marketing was concerned. What better way than a train full of people he could analyze to come up with a convincing argument for why Rousseau Belle should use his company?

The closest stop was only a block away, and Tristan took long strides toward it as he enjoyed the scenery around him. He sometimes forgot how beautiful Paris was, especially when work was so demanding. The well-kept streets and the trees lining the Seine. The older buildings gave character to the Paris skyline.

The smell of crepes wafted to him from around the corner, and he thought about stopping for one on the way. Seeing the long line, he continued on, ready to escape the heat of the July sun.

Taking the stairs down to the Métro, he enjoyed the change in air temperature which allowed him to leave his suit coat on. He'd worn a suit almost every day since he'd taken over the company, and while it wasn't usually uncomfortable, the summer heat made him wish he was at the beach rather than working.

With two gates to enter the train stop, he got in line behind a woman with light brown hair falling to the middle of her back, waiting for her to scan her card. After several attempts, the gate didn't open, and she pawed through her bag, looking for something.

Tristan pulled out his wallet, taking one of the tickets he kept for different situations and handing it to her. "Take this."

"Thank you," she said, stopping for a minute as she saw his face. He was somewhat used to that, being the CEO of a marketing company.

With his picture all over the city, it was inevitable that he'd get at least one comment each time he went out.

Her bright blue eyes drew Tristan in, awakening a curiosity inside him. She shook off the hesitation and said, "I seem to have grabbed one of my old cards today." She inserted the ticket into the machine and waited for it to pop back out. Nodding again to Tristan, she took long strides down the tunnel, looking back only once.

"Are you getting on the train, or are you just going to hold up the line staring at a girl?" The man's voice from behind him was frustrated, and Tristan tapped his own card on the reader and strolled down the hall to the platform, grinning as the guy barreled past him and onto the train platform. He had enough to worry about besides a girl with crystal-blue eyes.

Glancing around the platform, he gave his mind free rein, starting an analysis of what he could learn about the people near him. Although the outside appearance couldn't tell him everything about a person, it could tell him enough to get a jump-start on what might interest them in ads.

For the dog owners, he could picture different magazine spreads and television commercials about the latest dog food, collar, or costume. For the men, it was either sports, beer, or video games. As he looked at the woman next to him, he tried to figure out an angle to pitch to her, but his brain came up empty.

Forcing his analysis, he saw a simple engagement ring on her finger, with limited jewelry in her ears and a touch of makeup on her face. Maybe a mid-tier piece of jewelry? A focus on a simple makeup routine? Angela was right. He did need a lot of work to figure out what women would need in order to focus advertising on them.

As he scanned the train platform, he noticed the woman from the turnstile standing at the far end, tapping her foot as she looked up and down for the train. She glanced at her watch, and it made him wonder what she was late for.

At this distance, he studied her. She was beautiful, with a slightly upturned nose and bright pink lips. He was too far away to see her eyes as clearly as he had up close, but her tall, slender form surprised him, as she had only been a few inches shorter than his six-foot-one-inch frame, and her heels didn't add much height. Dressed in a black skirt with a light pink blouse, the only thing she carried was a large shoulder bag.

With no jewelry on, she wouldn't be the type of person to need a diamond commercial, but with how fast her foot was tapping, she could definitely use a massage or something to loosen her up. She'd seemed nice enough at the entrance to the platform, but he didn't know if it was out of embarrassment or just her personality.

The train finally arrived, bringing a gust and the smell of brakes with it. Tristan waited for the other passengers around him to step on before he entered through the door. Taking a place right next to it, he held on to one of the rails from the ceiling, spreading his feet to brace himself as the train took off.

The destination he was waiting for came three stops later, and when he got off, he realized the woman with the bright blue eyes had as well. She turned and walked in the other direction as they emerged from the exit, though; he shook his head, trying to clear her out of his mind as he walked to the office of the skin care company.

CHAPTER 4

Juliette couldn't get her heartbeat to slow down to its normal pace. She couldn't believe that Tristan Delacroix had been standing behind her to get on the train. Was it because she'd been mentally criticizing him all morning as she passed one ad after another? If that was any indication, he was thorough. If she did let his company take over advertising for her, her logo would be everywhere.

When she got off the train and saw he'd done the same, her curiosity took over, making her wonder what he was doing in that part of the city when his business was near the Eiffel Tower.

Instead of heading straight for her office, she'd veered to the right, remembering she needed to pick up something from the printer.

Walking into an office building about a block from her office, she waved to Sabine, the receptionist, setting down the bag of things she'd picked up on her rounds.

"How are you today, Juliette? I've got the samples you requested right here." Sabine moved from behind her desk and handed Juliette a brown paper package. "Just call and let us know if those work. Jean-Marc said we can change where it sits on the labels a bit if you don't like how it's placed now."

Nodding, Juliette said, "Thank you. Once I've approved the design, what is the turn-around time for about five hundred?"

Holding up a finger, Sabine walked behind her desk again and flipped through a few papers. "We don't have as many printings scheduled next week, so probably two to three days. We have some things for Delacroix Marketing, and then we can put you on the press after that."

Juliette groaned internally. What were the odds that even her printer worked with Tristan?

"Thanks, Sabine. I appreciate it as always." She waved as she walked out the door and down the street, juggling all of her wares as they weighed her arm down.

She stood at the light, waiting to cross back, and took out one of the printed samples that would go on their new lip balm containers. Examining it carefully, she tried to see if there was anything that needed to be changed. She would have to put it up to the containers to make sure the typesetting and font size worked out, but instead of pondering those details for too long, her brain called up a picture of Tristan's chocolate brown eyes as he handed her a ticket.

Was she going crazy? Because Tristan Delacroix was out of her league. She needed to get back to work and stop thinking about the tall, handsome man who'd saved her an embarrassing situation just twenty minutes before.

CHAPTER 5

Tristan pushed open the door to Rousseau Belle, noticing the calming music and the brightness of the place. Everything was white, from the walls and furniture to the tile on the floor. Here and there were touches of color, but for the most part, it reminded him of a better-smelling hospital.

A woman behind the front desk stood and smiled at him. "May I help you with something?"

"I'm looking to speak with the owner. Juliette Rousseau?"

A moment of panic washed across the woman's face, and she replaced it with a softer smile. What would cause that? Was the Rousseau woman really that tough?

"Did you have an appointment?" She looked down at a notebook filled with scribbles and highlights. After flipping a few of the pages, she looked up when he hadn't answered.

"Sorry, I don't have one, but I just need five minutes of her time."

"Your name?"

"Tristan Delacroix."

Recognition dawned on her face, and she nodded. "I believe we already had someone from your company in just this morning. Is there something you wanted to add to the presentation?"

Folding his arms and leaning on the desk, he saw her nameplate said Rachelle Maret. "Honestly, Rachelle, I should have been the one to come and make the presentation. After learning of the outcome today, I wanted to make sure Ms. Rousseau knows exactly what we would be giving her company if she signed on with Delacroix Marketing."

Rachelle gave him a shy smile. "I don't know how much good it will do, but you can try to talk to her when she comes in. She had to run some errands and should be here shortly." The woman motioned to the chairs set up around a large carpet, and Tristan took a seat, making sure to face the door so he could catch the owner once she walked in.

A few minutes ticked by, and he checked his phone a couple of times, wondering if the receptionist had only made up an excuse to waste his time.

The door finally opened, and in walked a woman with light blonde hair, probably in her late forties. Dressed in a tailored business suit, she looked like she could be the owner, so Tristan stood, walking forward with his hand outstretched.

"I'm Tristan Delacroix. I was wondering if you have a minute to speak to me, Madame Rousseau."

The woman looked at him as though he'd gone insane. "I'm not Juliette Rousseau, but if you are mistaking me for the twenty-seven-year-old owner, that's quite the compliment. I'd say everything I've paid to this company to look younger has been well worth it." The woman smiled at him, and Tristan wanted to hide, the heat of shame rushing up his neck.

The woman behind the desk smirked, and Tristan swallowed, finding his mouth suddenly dry. "I apologize for bothering you. I'm just going to go sit over here." He took three long steps and sat back in his seat, doing his best not to look in Rachelle's direction. That was all he needed, to feel self-conscious when he would have to turn on the charm for whoever was the owner.

Rookie mistake.

He hadn't been this flustered since he'd graduated college and his father had assigned him one of the bigger accounts.

Pulling out his phone, Tristan put the company's name into the search engine, and up popped several articles. As he clicked on the company's website, he found the "about us" tab and clicked on it. It took a moment on his phone, but as the image became clear, he recognized the young face, the crystal-blue eyes. His heart jumped as he recognized the woman from the Métro was Juliette.

From the little he'd studied about her on the platform, he knew he needed to come up with a better plan of persuasion. This wasn't going to be as easy as walking in with his good looks and a dashing smile. He'd struggled to figure out an angle to pitch to her on the platform, and he'd have to be more prepared if he thought he'd have a chance.

He read over the bio on her site and looked up the town she was from, Dinan. He'd been able to travel a lot in his life, but he'd only been to Brittany, the area in eastern France where the town was located, once. How did a girl from a small town come to Paris and start a fast-rising skin care business?

The door opened and in walked Juliette, not even glancing in his direction.

"Hey, Rachelle, did I miss anything? The market was so busy, and I had a hard time finding those ingredients for that new cream. Has research called about the lip balm yet?"

The girl behind the desk shook her head. "You didn't miss much, and no, I haven't heard anything from research. You do have a visitor to see you, though." She tilted her head in Tristan's direction, and Juliette turned, her mouth going slack as she realized who he was.

"Are you following me?" she asked, the edge to her voice causing a response to stick in Tristan's throat. Her eyebrows knitted together, and he suddenly felt nervous from her glare.

Tristan stood, buttoning the top button on his suit coat. "No. I just came to talk to you about—"

"I know what you're here for," she said, cutting him off. "Your assistant tried to persuade me to change my mind this morning.

When I saw you at the train, I didn't think your destination was to my business. Just save us both some time because my answer is still no."

"I just wanted to make sure Rose explained exactly what we can do for your company." Tristan set his jaw, not sure what approach he should take. He wasn't used to girls not falling all over him because of his good looks and fortune, and it made him tongue-tied. Not that he tried to play those cards often, but it certainly made a lot of his job easier. He'd learned the power of persuasion from his father, and it wasn't often that he felt things as out of control as he felt now.

She folded her arms across her chest and looked up at him, unamused. "Thank you, Mr. Delacroix, but we've been doing just fine as it is with our current marketing plan."

How had she known his name? He hadn't introduced himself, and she'd hinted at knowing him at the train stop. Maybe it was because his face was around Paris, whether in the gossip columns or on advertisements for the Delacroix company.

Her words "just fine" echoed in his mind, shaking him out of the fog. "Just fine? Not the best attitude for a growing business."

She shook her head and turned to walk down the hall behind the desk.

Tristan hesitated but decided to follow, walking down the hall as Rachelle called after him to stop.

Juliette turned into an office, and he was surprised at how bare and void of personal effects it was. He was no interior designer, yet he'd made sure to have art hanging on the wall and several pictures of his parents and friends spread throughout the office.

"I'm sorry to disappoint you, but there are a lot of things we have in place that are helping to bring in customers, and I have someone in-house do the marketing for me anyway." She sat behind her desk and removed several containers and bags of what looked like plants from her shoulder bag before sliding the bag underneath the desk.

Tristan leaned forward, hands on her desk, trying to get her to look up at him. When she finally did, he saw a light pink spot covering a section of her chin, and he was curious as to what had caused it. From that angle, it looked like a scar. Probably just a childhood injury.

Looking at her eyes, he asked, "How big do you want this company to be, Madame Rosseau?"

He watched as she thought about it for a moment. "I would love to see my products used throughout the world, to make a difference in the lives of the teenagers who need it. To help adults have clearer skin and, hopefully, lessen the scars caused by acne. But I know that will come in time. We've already grown significantly since we started the company, having moved into this office only a few weeks ago, and it's important for me to not overextend myself while still maintaining the high quality of the products."

"What if I tell you we can get you into stores throughout the world by the end of this year?"

She laughed, and it started out as a giggle, expanding to a sound coming from deep inside. Her eyes locked onto his and made him feel as if she could see right through him. "Mr. Delacroix, you do realize it's July, right? Being able to produce that amount of product and ship it out to stores would mean I'd have to hire people now, and a *lot* of them. The time to train them on the correct procedures would take time as it is. Seeing as how I grow a lot of my own products on my parents' property, there's no way I could suddenly increase quantities to start producing four or five times what we do now by the end of the year."

Tristan stood up straight, looking down at her with surprise. He sat down in one of the chairs across from her, amazed at the complexity of her business. As he thought about it, most of the clients he worked for could increase production within a few weeks, not taking months for the materials to be ready. "You grow some of your own ingredients?"

"If a product's going to have my name on it, I want to make sure it's the best. Sometimes growing the plants myself is the best way to ensure that."

"Okay, what if I say we can help you reach your goal of international sales in two years?"

She shook her head, causing the irritation in Tristan's chest to blossom. "I'm going to be frank. I don't know how much you can actually help us. I've researched your company, and from the masculine look of your website and portfolio, I doubt you'd have the experience and expertise to actually make a difference in our sales."

Heat shot up his neck, and he crossed his arms over his chest. "I've been in the marketing business from the time I could walk, Madame Rousseau. Please, enlighten me on how your advertising strategy would be better than anything we can provide for you."

The corner of her mouth turned up as if enjoying every moment of his discomfort. "Right now, I can send out a new product to some of the beauty bloggers and Quickstagrammers, causing sales to go crazy days after. I blog three to four times a week about different changes I make in my skin care routine and our processes to create each product, as well as client success stories we receive. We get a lot of good traffic from that, which equals sales. I have newsletters going out to people wherein I share several tips for better skin care. Now, tell me, what is it you would do for our company?"

Opening and closing his mouth, Tristan couldn't find the words. He'd never felt like this before, never had to worry about what to say, only focusing on swaying the person to his side in the past.

After several seconds, he said, "I think you're right."

Juliette's head turned, and she looked at him out of the corner of her eyes, as if not trusting the change in attitude. "I wasn't expecting that response from you, Mr. Delacroix."

Leaning forward on his knees, he looked up at her, noticing the rim of her iris was dark but the centers were very light, causing an ombre effect. He looked back down to his hands, trying to make it so the words would form as he wanted them to.

"We've been known for everything to do with sports, real estate, and other smaller marketing efforts. But there's a lot of potential in the beauty industry, and I think we could really help you out, provided that we do our homework and come up with a plan that will be tailored to you. It will be something new, and it will be a challenge for my staff, myself included. If you're willing, I think we could make a great team."

She paused as if considering his offer, giving him a slight leap of hope. With the first broad smile he'd seen all day from her, she said, "Come up with this plan, Mr. Delacroix, and we'll go from there. I'm not saying it's a yes, but I don't want something that's just a template from some other industry trying to fit my company."

Tristan grinned, knowing it would be a lot of work to change out everything, but he only needed enough for a pitch.

"I'll make sure my team gets working on it now. Can I contact you at the beginning of next week? Will that work for you?"

"I'm not going anywhere. We have a lot coming through the pipeline with the new line of creams coming out, so the next few months will be busy."

Standing and moving to the door, Tristan said, "Thank you for this opportunity, Madame Rousseau. I'll talk to you then."

She smiled at him, and even though it looked more like doubt in his abilities to pull it off, the determination to succeed filled him. A successful pitch for Rousseau Belle was going to be one of the biggest starts to a whole new industry for his company.

CHAPTER 6

"That went well," Rachelle said, bringing in several papers.

"I wanted to take a picture of his face when I told him no. I wonder how many times people have told him that in his life." Juliette laughed at the memory.

Rachelle grinned wide, her small laugh only fueling Juliette's laughter to continue. "Not enough, that's for sure. So what made you give him another chance?"

Juliette clicked the top of her pen a few times as she thought about it. In her head, she'd kept telling herself that there was no way she'd work with a guy like Tristan Delacroix, rich and full of himself. And when the words had popped out, she was stunned.

"I guess I'm curious to see what he could do for us. We've made good strides on our own, and with all the different avenues we've been working, things have gone great. But I don't want us to get comfortable. Trying new things will help keep this company thriving."

"I can understand that. Oh, Chris from research came looking for you while you were in the meeting. I think they wanted you to test out the new lip balms."

Juliette stood, feeling another wave of excitement run through her.

Research was one of her favorite parts of the business, seeing how just a few extra drops of one ingredient could make or break the formula.

"Why don't you come out and try it with me? It's always nice to have more than one opinion."

Rachelle squealed and clapped her hands together. "I love it when you say that. I'll go lock the front door. It's after hours anyway."

Waiting for her, Juliette thought over the two encounters she'd had with Tristan Delacroix today. She was grateful she'd been so flustered at the train gate that she hadn't said something lame or awkward. It hadn't been hard to recognize a face plastered all over Paris. When she'd seen him sitting in her office, she'd put everything together, realizing this was probably a last-ditch effort to get her business.

She thought of his tall frame, the dark brown hair styled to the side with a clean cut, thin beard. As much as she didn't want to admit it, she found him attractive, more so in person than in the media and ads.

"Mr. Delacroix's a dreamy guy, don't you think?" Rachelle's mischievous smile made Juliette laugh.

"Yeah, but can you imagine having to date an ego like that? He's probably one of those people who dictates what the girls he dates should be wearing."

Rachelle smiled. "I don't think I'd mind that. Especially if it's one of the name brands and he bought it for me. How can a girl turn down Chanel?"

Juliette turned and smacked her lightly on the shoulder. "Oh, please. What are you doing, fawning over someone in a different league from the two of us? Aren't you in love with your own Romeo?"

"Yes, Gillis is pretty amazing. But you never know where life could take you. Especially *you*. When are you going to start dating again?"

With a snort, Juliette said, "Again? When did I really ever date? You're lucky you met me after high school."

"I don't know why you look back at those times with such regret. I've seen pictures of you around that time. Your skin was just like most teenagers, and it wasn't that bad."

Juliette felt the burn in her face as she remembered all the days of hurt and sadness that summed up her high school education. The various times eating in the bathroom and dreading gym with the popular clique, hoping her makeup would hold up through the sweat dripping down her face. Even now, after years of clear skin and a successful growing business around skin care, those old feelings of being The Ugly Duckling crept up every once in a while.

Like when a handsome and successful man like Tristan looked at her in a way she'd never been looked at. But he was only trying to get her business, not date her.

"I can't remember exactly how bad it was now, but some of the comments have a way of sticking."

Rachelle nodded, turning slightly as they continued down the hall. "But think about it. Would you have done all you have to help people going through the same thing if you'd never had problems? Think of all the teenagers you're helping now so they won't have to be teased as much as you were."

With a smile, Juliette said, "That's a good point. I'm not sure. I probably wouldn't have been as passionate about it."

The reviews and feedback helped fuel her desire to succeed and progress. The young men and women who'd written to say their whole lives changed once their acne or rash had cleared up after using Rousseau Belle kept her going. Most had tried just about every other product on the market, and the compliments helped her feel satisfied after months of working long hours. Even Rosalie, one of the girls who'd ridiculed her to no end for years, had given her a five-star review about how she loved the products for their use and scent. In some ways, that was better than any revenge she could have planned.

Entering the prep room, Juliette pulled her lab coat from its hook, taking out a disposable hair cap. She gathered her long, thick hair, stuffing it inside the cap. Rachelle dressed similarly as any contamination would cost money in new supplies and the setback of time, both of which she didn't like to waste.

Three researchers stood behind a table set up with several samples. Chris, the research lead, nodded to her and Rachelle. "Thanks for coming out so late today. We thought about waiting for the tests until Monday, but we wanted to show you what we've come up with so far." He pointed to the small containers holding a cloudy gel-like substance. "We've finished the lip balms using the aloe vera with the different oils. It took longer than we projected to get the ingredient amounts right. The first test ended up too watery."

Juliette leaned over, picking up one of the containers. "These look great. We decided not to do any colors on these, correct?"

"We've been testing with the juices from fruits to make the color natural, but we still haven't come up with the right formula for them. An option would be to sell what we have here as one line of plain lip balms. When we figure out the other, we can sell it as something close to a lipstick."

Juliette scooped at the balm with her finger and swiped the cream across her lips. Rubbing the upper and lower lip together, she did her best to analyze it for things like texture and smell.

"I like this one. What's in it?"

"That one is just the aloe and some vanilla," Chris said, placing his hands behind his back. His smile was hesitant, and Juliette knew he was waiting for any and all feedback before celebrating their success.

"Okay, will you put some of each kind into little jars, and I'll try them out over the weekend?" After rubbing her lips together again, still feeling the smooth texture of the balm, she said, "Why don't each of you do the same? Look for how long it lasts. Does it soothe your lips, or does it dry them out in the long run? Is the smell bearable, or can you smell it at all? We'll come back on Monday and talk about what we found. That way we can make an informed decision about which to put into production and which ones we need to keep working on. Does that work for you all?"

The three researchers nodded, and one of them, Marie, moved to complete the request. Chris grinned. "My wife is going to love you even more than she already does."

Juliette laughed. "Well, make sure she tries them out too. The more real feedback we have, the better we can plan for when it launches." It was a common theme from her, but more often than not, it served to help her wait for the feedback before getting it out to production first thing.

Marie came back with two small sacks, each filled with five little pots of lip balm, handing them to Juliette and Rachelle.

"Thank you, everyone. Have a great weekend," Juliette said before turning back to the door.

As they walked back to the front, Juliette could see Rachelle rubbing her lips together.

"What's your initial reaction to it?" She valued the opinions of her employees, but Rachelle had been with her from the start, when Juliette had just moved to Paris with a dream and a few products. Rachelle accepted the position to be an assistant while still going through University and had stuck with Juliette since. She could give feedback without making Juliette feel like a failure while helping her bounce ideas to correct problems.

"I think this is a good product so far. Usually after just a few minutes, the typical lip balm is already grainy and dry. But this still feels like I just applied it." She grinned and held up the small bag. "Just one of the many perks of working at your company."

Juliette smiled. "Yeah, but I'm glad you're here. It's been a wild ride these past couple of years, and I couldn't have done it without your encouragement and help. Hopefully the next few continue on just as well."

"I'm hoping Mr. Delacroix comes through with a killer marketing design so you have to work with him."

Feigning like she'd been stabbed in the heart, Juliette said, "You want me to die? Seriously, working with that guy more than just a day would probably put me into a coma."

"I don't think he's that bad. Just because he has a lot of money and he's very attractive doesn't mean you shouldn't try to get to know him."

"Please, have you seen the girls he usually dates?" From Rachelle's raised eyebrows, Juliette realized what she'd just said and held up her hands, the bag she was holding moving back and forth with the motion. "Not that I've been keeping track, but from the pictures I've seen, they're on a whole other level."

Juliette grabbed her shoulder bag and waited at the front desk while Rachelle got hers. She sneezed and then sneezed again, pulling a tissue from her bag.

Rachelle grinned at her and said, "You never know unless you give the guy a chance. Maybe he's sick of that type of girl, and you're the perfect combination of fun, beautiful, and chill. There are guys out there who would love to find a girl like you."

"Don't hold your breath, Rachelle," Juliette said with a chuckle. The chances of her clicking with Tristan Delacroix on a more intimate level were next to none.

Tristan's mind had gone into overdrive as he'd taken the train back to get his car at the office and then returned home. He decided that if he wanted to have a chance at the campaign, he needed to get the presentation put together by Monday. With a trip planned to visit his friend and frat brother, Jackson, in Australia in a couple of weeks, he wanted to make sure he had enough time to get the campaign started off right, if she decided to go with his company.

Although he'd thought about calling a last-minute meeting this late on a Friday night, he'd decided to take this one on by himself. His team had been spread so thin on several new campaigns as it was. Tristan just couldn't hire people with the experience they needed fast enough to keep the company rolling at the increased pace.

The fact that Juliette had even given him a sliver of hope was reassuring, and if he messed it up, he doubted she'd give him another chance. That was enough to drive him to succeed, to fulfill the expectations his clients had for him and make them fall in love with their marketing campaigns.

He could barely sleep that night with all the thoughts spinning in his mind. The next evening, pacing back and forth in the large penthouse he'd bought the year before, he tried to gather his thoughts, thinking of everything he knew about how to market to women. He'd already read through several articles, taking copious notes. But now, as he brainstormed, all of the tips sounded lame to his own ears. He needed to bounce ideas off of someone, and he thought about calling his father to do that, but knew they were probably just waking up while on their trip to California. They'd been traveling the world since his father's retirement, and Tristan already knew what his father would say.

"Why go after such a small company? The big money is where the big contracts are."

It was the main point of their disagreements over the years. Any contract, if given the proper attention and a good product to back it up, could be a big contract in just a few years. Tristan looked at each client as an investment into the company's future, which is why he needed an in for the beauty industry. Prove to the world that Delacroix marketing could help an up-and-coming business break into the beauty market, and he had the validation he'd need for future campaigns with new clients.

He'd been sitting behind a computer for hours on Saturday, the TV on in the background. Inspiration failed to come, even after several searches and articles on advertising to women. He'd done so many campaigns that focused on men, and the switch to something more desirable for women was making it difficult for his brain. He'd started four different proposals and made it to the halfway point before realizing it was just a copy of former campaigns, and they wouldn't impress Juliette.

After researching different Quickstagram profiles of beauty bloggers, as well as reading every article he could on the reviews, he stumbled across an interesting comment on one picture.

Y'all make it look so easy, like these products will work within thirty minutes of applying. But in my experience, most of these products take months to begin working. Who has months to see a difference or not see a difference? By then, we have to start at ground zero with the next line of products that supposedly keep us looking younger, going through this cycle over and over again until we die.

The comment triggered something in his brain. What if there was a way to show the differences? Short of having six months to try out all of the products and take pictures or video of it, there wouldn't be an easy fix to show future clients. They could try it for thirty or sixty days and make it into a challenge for users of Rousseau Belle. He wrote down those options and continued searching.

Tristan had scoured the website and Facebook page for Rousseau Belle, but he hadn't checked out their Quickstagram account. When he did, he was surprised at all of the different posts that could be used for his prior idea. Several of them featured Juliette's trial-and-error process, showing a lot of before and after pictures. He was surprised at how well she'd marketed herself since starting her company four years before. But he'd need to find even more avenues to bring her company business.

His phone rang, and Tristan smiled as he saw Jackson's name pop up. The two of them had gone through a lot together, leaning on each other when it seemed like the world had left them behind. Along with Roman and Evan, two members of their frat house in college, they were still close, working to build each other's businesses in different industries. Tristan knew their influence was a big part of why he has been able to grow his family's company to such heights in just a few short years.

"Jackson, what's going on?"

"Just got done surfing for the morning. Hailey and I are going on a hike later today, so wish me luck."

Tristan chuckled. From what he knew of Hailey after meeting her in California for her father's funeral a few months before, she was a firecracker and loved the outdoors. "Like you need that. What's up?"

"You're still planning to come to Australia in a couple of weeks, right? Hailey has a bridal shower sometime in there, and I'm hoping you'll be around so I don't have to go. Do you think I could call an emergency IBC club meeting?" Jackson chuckled at that, causing Tristan to do the same.

Tristan laughed more at the word "club" than him wanting all the guys to come in just for an excuse to get him out of an awkward situation. Since ten of the guys who'd been in their frat house were now billionaires, one of the guys had proposed they form the International Billionaire Club as a way to stay connected and help each other out.

With a snicker, Tristan said, "You want to set a date for two weeks out and have everyone make it to Australia to 'hang'? Good luck."

"Yeah, that's what Hailey said. I didn't sign up for the bridal showers. I just want to be married, T."

"Wow, is this really Jackson I'm talking to? Or have you been taken by aliens? 'Cause it sounds like she's got you whipped." Tristan chuckled at his own joke.

"Aw, come on, mate. I know how I was before. But I've never been so sure of anything in my life. Going from doing everything by myself to having someone to do it with all the time? Way better, mate. I can't even tell you what it's like. I'll gladly eat my words on anything I said about relationships and marriage before."

Resting his back against the couch once more, Tristan wanted to laugh the words away, like his good friend had been drinking bad water or something. But his chest seemed to rip open, loneliness filling the chasm. He was glad Jackson had found someone, since he'd been more of a rebel in college. If only Tristan could just skip forward to being in a relationship with someone already and not have to worry about the initial few dates of awkwardness.

"So things are going well with you and Hailey?"

Jackson chuckled. "I'd say so. She's already more familiar with the area than I am. Her real estate branch is taking off, and people love her. She misses her family a little bit, but I think she really loves it here. Besides the extreme heat."

"Yeah. I don't know how people can live there. I think I'll stay in Paris for a while."

"You're still coming, though, right?" Jackson asked.

It took a minute for Tristan to remember he hadn't answered the question the first time. "Yeah. I've got a lot of new things to implement for your company. Now that you're close to opening the store in California, we're going to need to train some people there too." He made a mental note to put that in his calendar. The store would be set up by the end of September, so he'd have to go or send someone in his place.

"That's why I pay you the big bucks. Just make sure we're actually earning something." Jackson laughed, and Tristan followed.

"I will, duh."

"Well, make sure you to bring your swim trunks when you come. We've got to get you surfing finally."

"You tried for years while we were at Hawthorne. When are you just going to admit I'm a lost cause?" Tristan laughed. No matter how many times they'd tried to teach him, he couldn't quite grasp the concept of riding on a piece of plastic over giant waves. Many people didn't think it was possible to get injured from a slow wave, but Tristan had always managed to do just that.

"Nah. It's like you trying to get me to wear business suits all the time. It's too hot for that." After a pause, Jackson said, "What about girls for you, T? Anyone tamed that cold heart of yours yet?"

For some reason, Juliette's face popped into his mind, her blue eyes keeping him in a trance. "No. No girls yet. Just one who is trying to get me to jump through hoops to get her business."

"Hmmm, that one sounds promising, then. Good luck, mate. Let me know when you're getting in."

Tristan hung up, his feelings mixed about the conversation. If Jackson could find someone who would love him after all of the ups and downs in his life, surely Tristan could too, right? He thought of his last relationship, which ended at the end of his freshman year when his then-girlfriend, Camila, married one of his best friends while he was off at college. Jackson had gone through something similar when his girlfriend dumped him because he wasn't going into the NFL.

Since then, Tristan's life had been work and more work, only dating when he was required to attend an event. He'd gone to the Mission: Adopted gala while he was in California to support Jackson and had regretted taking a date at all. A more recent headline emphasized that he'd taken one of the councilman's daughters out a few weeks back, and now everyone was speculating as to whether the playboy might be settling down.

He'd never corrected anyone on it, but he'd never enjoyed that nickname. A typical playboy would be out at the clubs or a bar instead of sitting inside on a Saturday night, trying to come up with an idea for work.

His thoughts drifted back to Juliette. There was something about her that reminded him of his ex-girlfriend. Maybe it was the curve of her mouth or the intensity of her eyes that reminded him of Camila. He pushed her out of his mind, done with dwelling on the past. He'd have to find a way to work with Juliette no matter who she reminded him of. She held the key to the future expansion of his business and, by extension, his success.

CHAPTER 8

Juliette spent the weekend sick in bed, but she was grateful she felt well enough to go to the office on Monday, knowing the next shipment of new cream containers had come in. The last time she'd received a shipment, most of the bottles had been broken, and she hoped there wouldn't be another delay for the same reason this time. She had a large order shipping to Berlin that week and didn't want to have to send an apology to the buyer.

Arriving around ten in the morning, she was surprised to find Tristan waiting for her already.

"Have you been waiting long?" she asked more to Rachelle than Tristan.

Rachelle leaned in and said in a whisper, "He's been here since I got here about 8:30."

Leaning over the counter, Juliette frowned and said, "Why didn't you call me or at least tell him to come back?"

"Well, I knew you were sick and didn't want to rush you. I told him to just come back, but he said he didn't mind waiting." Rachelle gave Juliette an exaggerated smile, her eyes almost invisible as they beamed at her. She pointed to the guy sitting on the couch.

Turning to Tristan, Juliette let out a loud sigh. "Okay, worm catcher. Come on, let's get this over with." She took long strides to her office where she dropped her bags next to her desk and opened the top drawer. Pulling out a bottle of aspirin, she took a couple before washing it down with water from her water bottle.

Tristan stood at the door with an odd expression, and she motioned for him to sit in the chair in front of her. "Worm catcher? What is that supposed to mean?"

Juliette chuckled, having already forgotten she'd said that. "Oh, one of my friends always used to say, 'The early bird catches the worm.' We shortened it to worm catcher." She looked him up and down, admiring his look in a tailored black suit. He definitely filled it out nicely. Shaking her head, she said, "You didn't have meetings or anything at your office you needed to take care of today?"

"The benefit of being the boss is that you can delegate. I chose to do that this morning." A hint of a smile played on his lips, and Juliette looked toward her computer screen to keep from staring. That was the last thing she needed to be doing, ogling the guy she was trying to get rid of.

"Okay, what have you got? I'm actually surprised you have something so soon."

A wide grin brightened his face, and his eyes softened, as if he'd already gotten the go-ahead for the project. The beard looked as though a professional had trimmed it, and for some odd reason, Juliette wanted to run her hands over it to see if it was as soft as it looked.

No, no, no. She needed to focus on the presentation so she could be done with him.

"I couldn't let this chance go, so I wanted to make sure I got the information to you as soon as possible."

He handed her a folder, and Juliette was surprised when she opened it to find colorful charts, pictures, and a list of ideas. She did the best she could to keep her face neutral, not wanting to give away too much when talking business.

Once she had looked through all the pages, she lifted her gaze to his and said, "Now that I've seen what's in here, I would like to hear what your vision is for this company."

Tristan opened his mouth to speak, but Juliette's phone started to ring. Looking over, she saw it was her mother and groaned.

"I completely apologize. I don't usually do this, but this is my mother calling, and if I don't talk to her now, she will literally not stop calling until I answer. Just give me a minute."

"No problem," Tristan said with a smile, his deep voice rattling around in her chest and making her head fuzzy.

She couldn't believe he'd already waited for an hour and a half, and now she was making him wait longer. Then again, she didn't really mind. He was the one pushing to meet with her.

Walking out into the hall, she answered the phone. "Hey, Maman."

"Juliette, we need you." Her mother's voice sounded frantic, and Juliette held her breath, hoping it wasn't bad news.

"What's wrong? Is everyone okay? Did Papa have another heart attack?" Her heart sped up, and she hoped no one had died.

Her mother sniffed, and Juliette wished she'd just spit it out. "We just came back from the doctor for his first checkup. He said your father can't do anything strenuous for the next month. The festival is three weeks away. He hasn't even finished half of the inventory he usually makes since most of it was sold at the arts festival a few months ago. Please, Juliette. We won't be able to survive the winter if you don't come home." The words sounded broken, and Juliette's heart leaped.

Guilt filled her as she thought of everything she needed to finish in Paris, mainly to get the launch of several new products ready. She hadn't had time to follow up with the researchers about the lip balms yet, but that might have to wait. "So he can't do anything?"

She really hoped her mother would say she was joking and that she just wished Juliette would make it to the medieval festival to be held in their small town in a few weeks. She'd missed the last one and hadn't been home except for the month before when her father had a heart attack. The thought deepened her guilt. But by the worry in her mother's voice, Juliette doubted there was any joking going on.

"He's just supposed to rest and take it easy. The stress of the festival can…" Her voice trailed off but Juliette knew more stress only heightened the chances of another heart attack.

"Let me see what I can do, and I'll come out as soon as I can. I'm sure Rachelle can handle most of the operations from here."

Juliette's thoughts were tied up in all the things she'd need to rearrange, when her mother said, "You'll bring your boyfriend this time, right? We still haven't met yet, and it might cheer up your father to meet the man you've been spending so much time with."

"Maman, you're worried about seeing my boyfriend right now when Papa isn't doing well? Can't it wait?" Leaning against the wall and sinking down to her heels, Juliette put her head into her hand, feeling sick again. She'd told her mother four months ago that she'd started dating someone but had been vague in the details, hoping she could keep up the ruse for a while longer and avoid lecture after lecture about being alone.

"If you're serious about him, wouldn't it be good to have him here with you, comforting you?"

Biting her bottom lip, Juliette said, "He has to work too. It's not like he can take off weeks at a time. With the festival in three weeks, there's no way—well, it's hard enough for me to get away for that long, let alone him."

When she heard her mother's voice again, it was soft, almost pleading. "There's no harm asking, though, right? Even if he only has a few days he can spend with us, it would be better than nothing. And your father, who knows how much longer he has left."

Juliette felt as if a knife had sliced right through to her heart. Nothing like the Rousseau family guilt to change a mind. Closing her eyes, she said, "He had a heart attack, Ma. He doesn't have cancer."

Her mother took in a sharp breath, and Juliette knew she'd said the wrong thing. "Don't act like that about your father's condition, young lady. Who knows if he could catch something now that he's in a weakened state. Please just tell me that you'll bring him."

"Fine. I'll see what I can do."

Clapping echoed over the phone, and Juliette remembered Tristan was still waiting for her in her office. "I've got to go. I've got a meeting. But I'll let you know my plans."

"Thank you, dear. I knew you'd come through for us. I'll get everything settled for the both of you." It was just like her mother to be happy after finally getting her way.

CHAPTER 9

$\mathcal{H}$anging up, Juliette groaned, knowing she could only blame herself for this mess. What was she going to do? Why had she told her mom she was dating someone? She'd thought it was the greatest plan ever for the past four months, giving a couple of details about him here and there and then not getting the lecture about how she was throwing her life away on a career instead of becoming a mother and wife. It wasn't as though Juliette didn't want those things. The opportunity just hadn't presented itself quite yet.

Turning off her phone, Juliette stood and trudged back into her office to sit in her chair, feeling like her body was composed of lead. With her mind miles away, she turned to Tristan and said, "I'm so sorry. Go ahead with your pitch."

He started talking, and the richness of his voice seemed to lull her into a trance. She studied his face and saw his excitement about whatever it was he was explaining. When he pointed to things in the folder, she somehow managed to turn to the pages he wanted to reference, but she still heard next to nothing, numb to the fact that she'd have to reveal her lie to her parents or come up with a better temporary solution.

When Tristan finished talking, it was like her ears unclogged, and she heard him say, "What do you think?"

Uh. "Sounds like you've done a lot of research, and I appreciate that. I'm still a little hesitant because this is such a big step. We'd basically be your guinea pig for the beauty industry."

"I understand. It's hard for a lot of people who are so close to their business to trust someone else to care about that business just as much as they do."

She was glad she was sitting down because the look on his face made her almost sigh out loud. His eyes made him look like one of those adorable Beagle dogs, and she half expected him to kneel on the ground and start whining like one.

He is good. How is someone supposed to say no to that?

Shaking her head, she rubbed her lips back and forth, grateful for the application of the new lip balm to keep her mouth from feeling like a desert.

What was her deal? This was the Playboy of Paris, the billionaire who moved in circles she couldn't even imagine associating with.

As she looked at him, biting her bottom lip, a thought came to mind. What if he agreed to be her fake boyfriend? He could come with her for the three weeks until the festival and convince her parents that she'd had a boyfriend, and then she could make up some excuse in a couple more weeks as to why she'd broken up with him. Then, technically, it wasn't like she "wasn't trying" but that she just didn't have good luck, at least in her parents' eyes.

"Are you all right?" Tristan asked. "You look a little pale."

"Yes. Oh, well, actually no. I seem to find myself in a situation I had hoped would never happen. I have to go to Dinan, where I'm from, for a few weeks to help out my family for a big festival we have every other year. My dad is an artist, and the festival is a good boost to their income, helping them put money away for extra expenses and such."

"Okay." The look on his face told her he still didn't understand what her deal was.

Feeling as though she needed to explain more, she said, "With my father's health, they aren't sure how much longer he'll be able to work.

He had a heart attack several weeks ago so every bit helps." Why had she said that? It wasn't like he needed the rundown on her family, unless he agreed to be her fake boyfriend. Maybe knowing the details would make him more sympathetic to her predicament.

Trying to decide if she was actually going to ask him, she took in a deep breath, and the words spilled out. "I may have lied to my parents and said I had a boyfriend, and now they are demanding I bring said boyfriend home to meet them. My mom is convinced my father will die at any moment and that bringing home someone will heal him. I know how it sounds." She bit her bottom lip as she studied his face.

The smile on Tristan's face told her he was enjoying this moment. She pictured him leaning back with a bucket of popcorn, tossing some into his mouth. "You told your parents you're dating someone, and you're not?"

Juliette sat a little straighter, frowning at him. "It's not like I don't have the opportunity to have a boyfriend," she said, feeling defensive. "You don't know my mother. She can lecture a wall and make it move if she had to."

"What are you going to do, then?" he asked, studying her as though she were some oddity in a museum.

Leaning forward, Juliette clasped her hands together on the desk. Closing her eyes for a minute, she tried to focus before she opened them and looked directly into the dark brown irises of the billionaire.

"I feel really weird even asking this, but I was thinking I could contract someone to be my boyfriend, just for a few weeks." Staring into the chocolate pools of his eyes, she said, "How bad do you want this contract with our company, Mr. Delacroix?"

For a moment, he looked more panicked than she felt, and it made her smile that both times she'd seen him, she'd been able to wipe off the swaggering smile he always seemed to wear. Where was his popcorn-tossing smirk now?

"Well, Madame Rousseau, you would help our company grow by breaking into the beauty industry, but I'm a little nervous about what you're going to ask me right now."

"If you agree to be my fake boyfriend for three weeks, the contract is yours."

Tristan's face flickered with several emotions, and Juliette sat with her hands clasped tightly, more embarrassed as the seconds continued to tick by. She hadn't thought to ask him if he already had a girlfriend; although, with all of the media on him, it would have been a newer development since she hadn't heard about one.

He stood, walking back and forth in her small office, one hand raking through his hair. Finally, he turned to her, leaning on the back of one of the chairs. "So, I just have to go to your parents' house and be the doting boyfriend, and then you'll let my company do the marketing for yours?"

Blowing out a breath, Juliette said, "Yes. Just play the part of my boyfriend for at least three weeks, until the festival. If you have to leave for work stuff, it's not the end of the world. But at least they'll have met someone and I won't look like a total…well, I won't have to suffer through another lecture from my mother."

"Okay, I'll do it."

Raising her eyebrows, Juliette said, "You will?" She couldn't believe he would agree to something so quickly. She'd underestimated the weight that contract held in his mind.

"Yeah, I've always wanted to see Brittany, and the time away might be good for me. I haven't taken much time off in a while. When would we need to leave?"

Juliette took one of her business cards from the pile on her desk and pushed it toward him. "It looks like I've got your contact information on this folder, so when I figure out the details, I'll contact you. I'm hoping to have everything wrapped up today and organized for the time I'm gone so that I—I mean, we can take one of the trains in the morning."

"That should work. Do you need to debrief me or should we set some rules on this whole thing, Madame Rousseau?"

Juliette paused, trying to decide. She could see he was more than anxious to leave and finally said, "To start with, call me Juliette, or

Jules. If you call me Madame Rousseau, my parents will be suspicious."

"You can call me Tristan." He smiled at her as though this was the most ridiculous conversation ever.

Juliette looked down at the desk, composing herself to say what came next. But she realized that talking about the limits of kissing and touching was not something she was prepared to do right then.

"The train ride is over three hours, so we'll have time to talk about other rules and information on the way." She paused for a moment, debating whether or not to ask the question. "Do you have a girlfriend we need to notify about this?"

One of his eyebrows went up, and his smile looked hesitant. "I do *not* have a girlfriend."

"Good to know." Juliette nodded, as if he'd passed some unknown test. A thrill shot up her back, and she had to work to keep her face neutral.

"Okay. See you tomorrow, I guess." His smile looked more forced as he waved on his way out of the room. As soon as he was out of sight, Juliette collapsed in her chair and moaned.

Rachelle ran in, hovering over her. "What happened? Are you okay?"

"I may have just asked Tristan Delacroix, billionaire playboy, to be my fake boyfriend. He agreed."

Rachelle frowned, a mixture of confusion on her face. "Wait, what? Why would you do that?"

"My mother." Instead of a confused look, Rachelle smiled wide and nodded as if that were a totally acceptable answer.

"What did he say? I mean, he said yes, but did he say anything else?"

With a half-frown, half-stare, Juliette said, "He said yes and asked if we needed to set some ground rules. What guy in their right mind would say yes to a fake relationship?"

"One who really wants your business, I guess," Rachelle said, laughing. "Ground rules might be a good thing. Then you won't be caught off guard by anything weird."

"Well, then he'll be putting in a lot of effort for that contract, because visiting my family is no picnic." Juliette paused, her brain going a mile a minute as she tried to process it all. Cocking her head to the side, she looked at Rachelle. "You think I need to worry about ground rules? I mean, the guy just ran out of here like he was going to throw up."

Rachelle grinned. "I may not know the guy, but from what I've read about him, he doesn't do second dates. With *anyone*. Maybe he's just a little nervous about a long-term relationship."

"Please. Three weeks is long-term? At least it won't be real. I'd have to play second fiddle to his ego."

Even as the words were coming out of her mouth, Juliette knew they were the truth. Now she just had to make sure she prepped him for the windstorm that was coming.

CHAPTER 10

$\mathcal{W}$alking out of Rousseau Belle, Tristan knew he would be useless at the office, and he didn't want it getting out that he was fake dating someone. Roman, Evan, and Jackson would roll with laughter when they found out about this.

Tristan had heard of people being desperate enough to hire a fake boyfriend or girlfriend, but he never thought someone would ask him to do that. Nor did he expect himself to accept. He still wasn't sure why he had said yes. It wasn't like her company was his last chance to land a contract with a beauty company, but something about those crystal-blue eyes seeing right through him made it seem as if she needed this more than he needed her business.

That's what this was, a service for a girl in distress. It was as close to playing the hero as he'd ever get.

Pulling out his phone, he dialed Angela as he pulled out of his parking spot.

She answered on the second ring. "Hello, Tristan. Are you taking the day off?" Her words were accusatory, as if he should have informed her much earlier than now.

"I wasn't going to, but I am now. I'm going to need to rearrange a few things from now until I leave for Australia." He hoped she wouldn't press the situation, but it was inevitable.

"Okay, rearrange as in what? Cancel meetings? Are you finally taking some time off?"

Sighing, Tristan debated whether or not he should tell her the full situation, knowing she'd probably analyze it for some underlying feeling he didn't have. At least he didn't think so.

"I'll be heading to Dinan for that time." He heard the pause on the line and did his best to navigate the roads around him, just wanting to make it home.

"Dinan. You don't have family there. What would take you that way?"

Tristan groaned. She was going to keep asking until he told her. "Juliette Rousseau has family there. In order to get the contract with Rousseau Belle, I'm posing as her fake boyfriend while she takes care of her family business because her father had a heart attack." He had to breathe in deeply after that sentence, grateful he'd been able to get it all out.

He heard clapping hands and a laugh. "This is amazing. I'm surprised you agreed to it. I guess you're willing to do whatever it takes to get that contract."

"Not whatever. We'll have some rules to abide by. This is just business, so don't go getting it into your head that it's anything different." Tristan was basically shouting at his dashboard, and Angela's laugh only got louder.

"I'll start working on shifting some of your duties to the other employees. They'll be excited to not have you standing over them as they work."

Shaking his head, Tristan tried to let the comment roll off. "Fine. Oh, and I'll still need to head to Jackson's in two weeks and get things set up there. Will you make sure to book the flights there? I'll only need to be gone a week for that." He had forgotten to tell Juliette about that. She would just have to make it work as he couldn't put the trip off any longer.

"Will do, Tristan." She paused, and he was about to hang up, when she said, "Just have some fun. It might not be the ideal vacation you've been needing, but at least a change of scenery will help you out, I hope."

"I'll try, Angela. Thanks again, and I'll call you when I arrive. I'm hoping someone has wifi there so I'm not completely off-grid."

They hung up, and Tristan's mind seemed to rev into gear, taking off at all the situations that could happen over the next three weeks.

What would her parents think of him? He'd only been introduced as the boyfriend to one set of parents in his life, and that had been nerve-wracking enough, even though he'd known Camila since he was young. What would it be like to fake meet someone's parents? He just hoped he had some thread of acting skills to not make it awkward.

Several times, he wondered if this was even worth it, if he should bother with her plight and just stay in Paris to keep working on his business. But there was something about her that pulled him in, and he wanted to know what exactly had driven her to fake having a boyfriend. What caused a beautiful woman to have to fake a relationship when she could be asked out by men everywhere?

What rules did he want to set in place? This was a business contract, and he had to keep looking at it like that. Define all of the unknowns up front, and it would make for less awkwardness in the moment. He just hoped he wouldn't have to divulge all of his sordid past, because even the thought of it made his tongue go dry and his chest ache.

Turning the car around, he made his way toward Éclair du Gâteau. He was going to need sugar to wrap his mind around the whole situation.

CHAPTER 11

Just after lunch, as Tristan stood on the platform for the commuter train, he tried to come up with anything he and Juliette had in common since it seemed they came from different backgrounds. The only thing he could think of was they were both the CEO of their companies. Something that drew him in about her was her business smarts. She seemed to care deeply about her company, making sure her products met a high standard of quality before being shipped to customers. The fact that she'd already been using social media and her website to get organic sales impressed him.

Maybe this trip would be a bit more exciting than most of the events he had to find dates for. If everything else failed, they could always talk about different aspects of their business. And it would give him more information to use in the different campaigns he would need to craft after this arrangement came to an end.

Glancing down at his watch, he saw it was five minutes to one with no Juliette in sight. Was it all a ruse for some joke, or was she just running late? He felt anxious, knowing he couldn't do anything about it. His Delta Phi mentor, Dan Montgomery, had taught him in college to arrive early to everything. Now, when things prevented him from being on time, it made his stomach turn into a twisted, knotted mess.

"Hey, sorry I'm so late. Things got held up at work with getting tasks sorted. I'm just glad I didn't miss the train." Juliette stood behind him and flashed a smile, sending a tingle down his spine. Maybe this wasn't the worst idea he'd ever had.

They boarded the train, and Tristan lifted their luggage onto the racks overhead.

"Thank you for lifting that. I'm tall for a girl, but I still struggle to put my bags up that high." She took a seat on one side while Tristan took the seat across from her. A table sat between them.

"Probably because your bag weighs a ton. What did you put in there? Books? Rocks?" He smiled at her and was rewarded with a light giggle.

She pushed a strand of hair out of her eyes. "Not really. I thought I did pretty well, considering I'll be there for three or four weeks and what I'll need to wear." She looked out the window as the train pulled away from the station.

Tristan pulled out a small notepad and pen from his laptop case. "So, we only have a few hours, and I have to know everything about your family. Are you ready to start talking?" He said it in a joking way and laughed when she pretended to fall asleep against the window.

"Are you sure you want to do this? Because when I think about my family, I'm pretty sure they're all crazy."

He watched as she crossed one leg over the other, noting that she wore relaxed jeans and a flowing top, very different from the business skirt and blouse from the day before. He'd chosen slacks and a polo, wishing he could wear something more casual but not sure if that would be best since he'd be meeting her parents for the first time.

"Too late now. We're already on our way." He grinned at her when she scrunched her nose trying to look mad. The corners of her lips turned up, and Tristan said, "Okay, so you obviously have a mom and a dad. What are their names?"

"Cyril and Mathilde. My grandfather lives with them, and his name is Robert."

"Mom's dad or Dad's dad?" Tristan asked, recording answers in the notebook. He'd have to study this later or he'd never keep all the facts straight.

"Dad's dad. I have three siblings. Mathieu and Henri are both married with kids. They usually come visit for the festival, but I haven't heard if they're coming or not this year. My younger sister, Isabelle, is an interior designer in London."

Tristan finished updating his notes before he looked at her. "So, why are you the one who has to come back and help with the business? Can't one of the others help out?"

"None of the others ever learned how to do it all. They learned some aspects of the business, but I spent a lot of time with my father, learning how to throw pottery and create the jewelry. The two boys have work and family, making it hard to come for an extended amount of time."

"And your sister?"

Juliette bit the bottom of her lip while picking at something on the tabletop. She finally lifted her eyes, and his stomach flipped at the cool blueness of them. They put him at ease, which was something he hadn't felt in quite some time.

"She's the baby. She was into ballet growing up, and that took a lot of her time, so I don't think she ever really learned how to do all the techniques."

Sitting back against his chair, Tristan studied her face, trying to get a read on her as a person instead of just a client he was trying to win over. She had a simple beauty about her, but even with small family troubles, she seemed happy and satisfied with her life. One question popped up that he couldn't find out from the analysis of her outward appearance.

"So why skin care? If you have all these artistic abilities, why pack up and leave to do something completely different?"

She looked as if she were in agony, and as he leaned forward and reached across the table, ready to tell her she didn't have to answer, she spoke. "I loved art and still do, but I found that with a little mixing of ingredients, I could change people's lives. And there were so many obstacles I couldn't break out of when I was home that I just needed a change, some kind of out. Aside from coming back when my father had a heart attack, I haven't been home in years, and I know I'll be put into those boxes the minute we arrive."

Simple enough. But there was still pain in her expression, and he wanted to ask her what the cause of it was.

Juliette sighed. "Tell me a little bit about you. I need to know more of your background to convince my mother we've known each other longer than two days." She smiled at him, only a trace of the nerves still showing on her face.

Tristan looked up at the train ceiling and then out the window, trying to decide what would be worth sharing with this almost stranger.

"I grew up in Paris, my dad sent me to college in the US—"

"Why would he send you all the way there?" Juliette interrupted. It wasn't an unusual question, as many of his friends had stayed in France or some part of Europe for university.

"Because it was one of the best programs for business. He had several friends send their kids there, and they're all very successful, businesswise." It had only been in the last few years that his father had explained the underlying reason was the need to get him away from Camila, and as betrayed as he'd felt upon learning that, he was now grateful.

Juliette leaned on the table with her head in her hand, staring at him. "Do you regret that? Do you wish you'd gone to school closer to home?"

Letting out a loud laugh, Tristan ran his hands through his hair and sat back. "I don't really know, honestly. I learned a lot there and gained some friends that I'll have forever. The mentor we had for our frat house was incredible and one of the reasons why so many of us have been successful in our own businesses."

He paused a second, debating whether or not he should tell her about his girlfriend marrying his best friend six months after he left for college. Or that his friends were also billionaires. He'd used that line a few times to gauge the kind of women he went out with. Most of them latched on at the thought of so much money. Which was why he hadn't dated anyone seriously since college. He didn't want to be loved for his money.

"I was mad at my father at first for sending me all the way over there. But in the long run, I don't think I'd be where I am without it. I was young and thought I knew exactly what my life needed. Turns out, I needed that shove to get started on what life was really like and to learn how to work hard through the obstacles to make something profitable."

"I guess the hard things in our lives can usually turn out to be the biggest blessings. But I only ever realize that after the fact, because during the trial, I'm hating every minute." She pulled out her water bottle and took a sip. "Do you have any siblings?"

"I had one brother who passed away when we were kids. He got really sick, and the doctors couldn't figure out what was wrong with him before it was too late."

Juliette's hand flew to her mouth while the other reached forward and touched Tristan's hand. The feel of her smooth skin on his sent volts of electricity flowing through his fingers and palm. "I'm so sorry. I can't imagine how hard that would have been."

"It was a while ago. I remember my parents being really sad for a long time, but I know I'll see him again eventually."

She went quiet for a moment, and her thumb moved back and forth along the back of his hand, soothing the faint ache from the loss of his brother.

Tristan moved his gaze out the window at the beautiful scenery passing. It had been some time since he'd been outside Paris with all the work he had going, but it was somewhat refreshing to see the landscape free from tall buildings and covered in bright greenery. Dinan was a small town, and he hoped the pace would be slower, allowing him time to reflect and refresh.

He finally turned back to her and asked, "So, when did you start your skin care company? You're only what, twenty-five or twenty-six?"

"Twenty-seven. I started playing around with different concoctions in high school. My father had some health problems around the time I took my end of level exams in school, so I gave up Unif to stay and work. I'd go down and throw bowls and plates and things, and in the evenings, I'd work on mixing creams and cleansers. I was always testing them out, wiping my newest concoctions on my family members to see how their skin reacted to it." She cracked a smile. "They learned to be on guard when I was around. Once I started to notice that some of the creams worked, I sold them to people around town."

"And why come to Paris?"

"Like I said, I needed to get out of all the labels and restrictions Dinan held for me. It's such a beautiful place, but I felt trapped there. I moved to Paris four years ago, and while it was a really exciting time for me, it was pretty hard for my parents since I'd helped with the business for so long. Isabella moved to London a few years ago after Uni, and I think being empty nesters is an adjustment."

"Did you ever regret leaving?" He wanted her to continue talking, inspired by her past and how she'd been able to grow a sizeable business through a passion. He'd always known he'd inherit his father's business, and while he loved the adrenaline rush of gaining a new client or seeing a particular marketing campaign take off, he might not have chosen it had it not been so available for him.

Juliette laughed, the sound deep and lovely. "No. It was a freedom like I'd never known, and I would do it a thousand times if given the opportunity. What about you? Have you ever wanted to live anywhere else?"

Tristan shook his head. "No, I travel enough that I'm satisfied with where I'm at." He paused a moment and then said, "Oh, I forgot to tell you. I have to fly to Sydney in two weeks. But I'll be back before the festival begins. Is that all right?"

He watched as she did the math in her head and nodded. "That should be fine. My mom will probably want to show you off at the festival, so if you can make it back by the first day, we should be good. I'll probably be heading back to Paris as soon as it's over anyway."

"What's the name of the festival again?"

"Fête des Remparts. It's a big medieval festival they've held every other year for years. The town goes all out with the costumes and decorations. There are booths to sell all kinds of medieval and modern items, and they have plenty of entertainment. The town of Dinan thrives on it, and it gives everyone a little bump in business."

Tristan's mouth dropped just a little. "Medieval, like knights and round tables and small village houses made out of hay?" He made sure to open his eyes wide and look like a small child bouncing up and down in his seat so she knew he was teasing. As a boy, he went through a phase where all he wanted to play was being a knight. His parents got tired of it after a while, offering him other options, but there was always something majestic and honorable about the knight. "I think my childhood would have been perfection had I been able to come to a festival like that. I loved everything to do with knights and battles."

"You've got the knights part right, and there might be a round table here and there, but our village isn't made out of hay." She looked him up and down, as if sizing him up for something. "I think you should enter the joust. It would be something you'll never forget."

"Horses and I aren't always on the best of terms. Can I just run at the other guy with the lance?" When she shook her head, he laughed. "I'm assuming we dress up?"

She nodded and said, "Oh yeah. Full armor if you want to be in the tournament. If not, it's just a bunch of robes." She paused, raising an eyebrow as she looked at him. "Are you all right? You look like you're having a hard time breathing."

Tristan chuckled. "I'm good. Just a little more excited than I thought I would be. Do I need to have a costume shipped to me, or is there somewhere to buy one in town?"

"The villagers in Dinan sell just about everything at this time of year, so I'm sure you'll find something suitable there." Tucking that stray piece of hair behind her ear again, she hesitated before saying, "How long have you been running Delacroix Marketing?"

"Seven years this September. My father had a heart attack, and my mother convinced him it was time to step back. He gave me the reins, and they've been traveling the world ever since."

Juliette's face turned thoughtful. "Do you miss them? Do you have other family here in Paris?"

Shaking his head, Tristan said, "My parents are from south of Paris, but everyone has passed away. I had a lot of love from my parents as I was their sole focus after my brother's death, but I'm not really sure what it's like to have a large extended family."

"Well, if my brothers and their families come, you'll be asking when the next train back to Paris leaves. They can get rowdy."

They chatted back and forth during the rest of the train ride, but Tristan still felt like he was in a dream. It seemed fate had smiled on him with a vacation, a contract, and a medieval festival all in one.

As they neared the station at Dinan, Tristan pulled out a chocolate bar from his suitcase. All he had to do was make sure he was the doting boyfriend, and it could all work out. Even chocolate wasn't enough to ease his nerves.

CHAPTER 12

The knot in Juliette's stomach tightened little by little as she got closer to her hometown. By the end, she had to hold her knee down so it wouldn't gallop away. She was pleasantly surprised that Tristan was so laid back. He definitely wasn't how most of the gossip columns liked to portray him, a brash businessman who could court a company for advertising but wasn't capable of keeping an intimate relationship with a woman. She just hoped he was a decent actor because there was going to be a lot of pretending to make their relationship believable to her family and, by extension, the community.

Now that she thought about it, no one was going to actually believe she'd snagged the attention of this godlike man before her. His strong jaw and chiseled features made it hard to keep her eyes off him. What had she been thinking?

That she needed a fake boyfriend and one who would be willing to do it for something she could give.

There was nothing she could do about it now. She just hoped her family would be somewhat normal and not divulge all of her most embarrassing stories. She might not have a future with this guy, but if she was going to work with him after this, she wanted to keep her dignity intact.

As the train approached the station, she was trying to wrap her fingers into knots, when Tristan reached out and pulled one of them away, his warm hand covering hers completely. She looked up at him, trying to read his expression, but saw a small smile. They barely knew each other, and she wondered what had caused him to hold her hand like that. Maybe he was practicing to make it less awkward in front of her parents. Whatever his intentions, she didn't mind it.

She shivered, and Tristan frowned.

"Are you all right? Do you need a jacket?" He turned to look around for something, not having anything handy.

"I'm good. Must have been the air conditioning or something." Looking back down to their hands, flutters filled her stomach, and she hoped the heat she felt in her cheeks wasn't obvious to him.

He must have seen her prolonged look at his hand because he said, "What's the consensus, skin expert?" The gleam in his eye told her he was teasing. "Some aloe vera lotion mixed with a vanilla scent?"

Juliette laughed, grateful to change her focus. "You could probably use one of my lotions, but I know a lot of guys are hesitant to have smooth hands."

"This is true. I've never been a fan of the greasy feeling that comes with lotion." The corner of his mouth turned up, and part of her wanted to lean over the table and kiss it off.

Turning, Juliette pulled a small tube out of her purse and handed it to him. "Try that. You won't lose your ego by using it."

"You think I have an ego?" he asked, a hint of teasing in his tone.

"Maybe. Just a little." After another pause, she looked at him and whispered, "Thank you."

He raised an eyebrow. "For what?"

"For coming with me. For being relaxed about the whole thing. For this." She moved her gaze down to their hands and then back up to his face. Wow, was she just tired, or did he look even more attractive than she'd thought before? It seemed as though with each layer she peeled back, she found more of him to like.

She needed to keep her distance. He'd probably break her heart if she wasn't careful.

Right before the train pulled into the station, she asked, "Are you really a playboy?"

As she studied his face, she wished she could pull the words back in. He looked like a wounded animal, and she was the one who had caused it.

"I'd like to think I'm not how the tabloids make me look. I'm so busy running a company, trying to make sure that all of my employees are taken care of, that I don't have time for dating much. Since there are pictures of me with a different girl at every event, they make me look like a heartbreaker."

"Why don't you date anyone twice?" She didn't know why she was asking him so many questions, but Rachelle's words had her curious. At least he'd been gracious and answered them for the most part.

Blowing out a breath, Tristan shrugged, but when he opened his mouth to speak, the train whistle went off, making it difficult to hear.

Juliette motioned to her ear and shook her head. "I can't hear you," she tried to say.

Switching seats, Tristan leaned in and whispered into her ear, "I guess I never found anyone I wanted to see more than once."

When he pulled back, Juliette couldn't pull her eyes away from his lips, the smell of his sandalwood cologne wrapping around her head. She looked up to his eyes and knew it was a mistake as her attraction to him grew even more.

Facing forward, she took a breath and then glanced back at him, the realization of what he'd said opening to her mind. "So, this is kind of a big deal, then?"

He nodded and slid down into his seat, his gaze fixed on some-thing higher up on the wall in front of them.

"I'm so sorry. But maybe if us being together gets out, you won't be the playboy anymore. Then again, I don't know how much they'll believe it after a month."

He seemed to consider that and nodded. "But it's a perk I hadn't even thought about."

"Do you want to get married?" Slapping her hand over her mouth, she wished she could just erase the last thirty seconds.

He narrowed his eyes, his mouth a tight line. "I'd sworn when I was in college that I wouldn't get married. But one of my good friends got engaged recently. I never thought I'd see the day when he'd get married, but they're planning a date and everything. We'll see how that turns out, though."

Juliette could see the tension in his jaw and wondered what had made him feel so deeply about matrimony. She wanted to ask more, but the train stopped, and they both stood, retrieving their bags.

Tristan picked up her laptop case and handed it to her before pulling down the suitcases from the rack. When she reached forward to take the handle of hers, he gently pushed her hand away and motioned for her to walk out the door of the train car.

She looked up with a curious expression. "What are you doing?"

"Playing the part of the boyfriend. I figured I should just do what I would normally do for a girl who I'd call my girlfriend. In this situation, I would carry her luggage." He raised an eyebrow as if waiting for her to contradict him.

"And holding my hand was—"

"To calm you down. You looked like you were going to twist your fingers together until they broke. It wasn't bad to practice, either, so we don't look as though it was our first time."

She nodded and turned, feeling a chill run through her. If she'd known she'd feel this way with a little attention from a fake boyfriend, she would have worked to find a real one sooner.

She made it to the door of the train and down the steps, turning to see if he needed help, to which he shook his head. Once he was on the platform, she said, "I thought you said you didn't have girlfriends."

He flinched, and she reached out, touching his arm. Not for the first time, she felt shame wash over her at her words. "I'm sorry. I'm just going to be quiet now."

Tristan shook his head. "No, you're fine. Just memories. Sometimes they hurt." His expression turned somber. He motioned in either direction, and Juliette realized she needed to lead him from there.

There was something about him going to college in America that he hadn't explained, but she understood the pain of the past he wanted to hide. No matter how many times she tried to tell herself she wasn't what the kids in school had always called her, the doubts would strike when she was most vulnerable.

She'd only met Tristan a few days before, and she didn't want to divulge the fact that her nickname back then was pizza face. Not that he was going to stick around after this arrangement was over, but she didn't want him to look at her with pity the entire time either.

Taking a big breath of the clear air, Juliette smiled, enjoying this moment and the familiar smells of Dinan. Not that Paris wasn't beautiful and clean, but there was something about her home, no matter how many memories it held, that would bring her nostalgia of the good times.

Turning back and forth to scan the train platform, she finally spotted her mother among the crowd waiting.

"This way," she said, leaning into Tristan so he would hear her over the train engine. He smelled so good, like rainwater and pine, but she had to focus. He didn't need to be creeped out by her for the next two weeks. "Get ready for the hailstorm."

"Huh?" was all Tristan said, but she'd already started to move away and didn't hear if he'd asked her to clarify.

Walking forward, she held out her arms and embraced her mother. "Hello, Maman. You didn't have to come get us."

"Nonsense. And make you walk all the way to the house with all your things? How would that have looked after you haven't been home longer than that short trip several weeks ago? We need to keep you coming back more often." Her mother's round face split with a grin.

Juliette looked around, hoping to see her father. "Is Papa at home?" As much as she wanted to see him there, she knew he needed to rest.

"Yes, I left him with your grandfather. I have some food simmering on the stove, so we should probably hurry back so they don't burn down the house." Her mother looked over Juliette's shoulder and smiled at Tristan. "Oh, Juliette, dear, did you really bring someone with you? Your father and I were convinced you'd made him up."

Heat rose to Juliette's cheeks, and she couldn't look Tristan in the eye at that moment, since she'd caught a glance of curiosity on his face. "Thanks a lot, Maman. This is Tristan. He's from Paris as well. Tristan, this is my mother, Mathilde."

Her mother pushed past her, approaching Tristan. Placing her hands on his shoulders, she leaned on tip toe and kissed each cheek. "It's so good to have you here, especially to know that you've been taking care of our daughter. We worry about her being alone in the big city, and…" Her mother leaned in, speaking so softly Juliette had to strain to hear her words. "We would like some more grandchildren soon. I've been worried she'd turn into our old maid."

"Maman!" This was such a bad idea. Normally, she endured the ridicule alone, but with an attractive audience, she didn't know if she'd survive this trip.

Tristan gave the traditional kiss on each cheek and stepped back. "She's an amazing woman, and she keeps me on my toes; that's for sure." He winked at Juliette, and she couldn't stop herself from smiling.

If only this were real.

"Just remember she gets all the good qualities from me." Her mother tapped Tristan's hand as if conspiring with him.

Turning on her heel, Juliette walked in the direction of the parking lot. Why hadn't she thought through this plan? She figured it would be so simple, that she could fool her family and go about her life like nothing had changed. The next two weeks were going to be pure torture as her mother was already falling over herself for a man who would never be Juliette's boyfriend in real life. Juliette's heart would be broken by the end of this, and it wouldn't just break her. She saw wedding bells in her mother's eyes.

If only her mother hadn't set an invisible timeline for when she had to complete each milestone in her life. Marriage was something she'd always dreamed of, but it was only recently that she could even consider it. When this was over, she'd need to date a lot more than her twice-a-year blind dates if she really wanted to settle down.

Once they got to the older van her family used for the company, Juliette cringed, knowing Tristan probably had some amazing car at home, or even several, with all the money he had. Getting into what her parents affectionately called Betsy was going to be a humbling experience for Juliette.

"Let me open the van for you, dear." Her mother pushed the button to unlock the doors, still excited about the remote even after ten years. The van had been the only brand-new purchase her parents had ever bought, and to this day, her mom still felt fancier because she had a remote control fob.

Juliette pulled open the back doors, to see the boxes of clay stacked several high. She went to grab her bag from the ground, but Tristan pulled it out of her grasp and lifted it with ease to sit alongside his in the van.

She gestured for him to take the front seat, but he refused, opening the door for her and waving for her to get in. They only had jump seats open in back, as much of the room was used to transport the art and materials that kept the family afloat. He climbed in back, his face neutral as he pulled down one of the seats and sat down.

The back window was rolled down right next to Tristan's head, and Juliette wanted to close her eyes. The window had been broken for the last few years, probably since she'd moved to Paris. Even after she offered to pay to have it fixed, her parents had refused.

He buckled his seat belt and turned toward her, a big smile on his face. He could be a tool about the whole situation, could look at her and say a contract wasn't worth what she was putting him through. But he was kind and polite, making her wonder what he would do had there not been something she was hanging over his head.

Maybe this was the reason she hadn't ever dated more seriously. There was no way she could handle having to introduce her boyfriend to her family. Even after this fake relationship was over, she wasn't sure her constitution could handle it again.

"Juliette tells me you own an art business where you make all sorts of pottery and jewelry." Tristan's voice was a bit louder than normal, probably accounting for the rushing wind next to his ears.

Juliette smiled at him, grateful for his pretend interest.

At his words, her mother lit up. Her favorite thing to talk about was the business, aside from her family and whatever she'd made for dinner.

"Yes, dear. My husband started making bowls and other pottery years before we met, but it wasn't until Juliette was around five that his design started to become a little more popular. We began getting people who would say, 'My friend bought a set of bowls from you, and they're beautiful. I want a set as well.' So we figured we could do it full-time. There are bumps in the road for sure, but it has kept us all alive until now." Her mother smiled at him through the rearview mirror as she turned down one of the streets.

"She also told me about the festival, and I'm very excited to see how it turns out. I didn't even know there was a medieval festival here."

Her mother frowned, and Juliette braced for the barrage of opinions about to be put upon them. "I told the committee that they really need to do better at getting the word out. We get several thousand people every year, but we could get even more if we put out fliers and let people know a few months in advance."

They drove in silence for a few more minutes, and her mother asked, "What is it you do for work, Tristan? Didn't even catch your last name."

"Delacroix. I work in marketing and advertising."

Her mother smiled and nodded, but no outburst came that she knew who Tristan was. This was one time Juliette was grateful her parents lived in a relative bubble, knowing next to nothing about the world outside their small town.

"Maybe I could give you a few pointers for your business. Do you have an online website?"

Juliette laughed first, which caused her mother to laugh as well.

"We aren't the most technologically savvy people in the world. We have to call Juliette or Isabelle when we can't get the television to work, and they have to walk us through it. Kind of embarrassing, if you think about it, but I figure if we've survived this long, we must be doing something right."

"Well, while I'm here, I can do a few of those kinds of things for you. It will make it easier for people to find you, and then you could even start selling things online."

"Don't get too crazy. When she says they don't know much about technology, she means it." Juliette tapped her mother on the shoulder, trying to hide her smile.

Her mother grinned. "We still have a landline. I haven't brought myself to get a cell phone. Cyril, my husband, has one, but I think I'd either just lose it or end up putting it in something that would ruin it."

Tristan's deep laugh made Juliette laugh as well. He'd been pleasant and cordial to her mother and had even managed to look comfortable in the old beat-up van. Offering to create a website for her family's pottery business? He was going above and beyond. He deserved the contract already just for surviving the first introduction to her mother. She only hoped he didn't regret his decision after he'd met the rest of the family.

CHAPTER 13

Tristan had seen the look on Juliette's face as they'd walked up to the van, and he knew he needed to be chill about it. Sure, this was the first time he'd ridden in the back of an art-supply van with the window stuck in the down position, but he wanted that contract, and he could play the part to make it so. Part of him went out to Juliette, knowing there was probably a lot more history here than she wanted to admit. He'd just have to make sure he helped however he was needed.

Driving through the streets of Dinan, he was surprised to see how much it resembled some of the older towns he'd seen in England. White outsides with lumber trim and overbuilds sheltering the doors. It was as if he'd stepped back in time, making him excited for what was to come during the festival. There was nothing quite like knights and swordplay for him.

Mathilde drove a few more minutes before pulling down a short road and stopping next to an older residence, a charming little cottage covered in rocks. It was a beautiful sight, and with a bit more room in between houses than in Paris, Tristan found it easier to breathe.

Even though Juliette had tried to beat him to it, he pulled the suit-cases out of the van and carried them at the back of the line. She seemed fidgety anytime he did something like that, probably not used to having someone help her out. To be honest, he was a little rusty at it, but he did his best to think ahead, working through what he needed to do to be the doting boyfriend.

As they walked toward the door, he whispered, "Is this where you grew up?"

She nodded, her face like stone. He hadn't known her long enough to understand her emotions, but there was something she was scared of, and he hoped she'd be okay.

They walked in the front door and into a large family room. Several mismatched couches and chairs sat to the right, while to the left was the kitchen and dining area. The aroma of cooking beef filled the air, causing him to breathe in deeply. It had been some time since he'd had a home-cooked meal.

"Okay, we've set up your room with fresh sheets, Juliette. Tristan, you'll be staying in one of the boys' rooms on the floor below. We traded out the twin beds for queens last year when Juliette's brothers came to visit. Dear, do you want to show him where to put the bags?"

Mathilde smiled at the two of them, and he saw Juliette stiffen, reaching forward to grab on to her mom's arm. "Who isn't coming?"

"Mathieu and his family decided to stay at a hotel outside of Dinan. Avelline is still recovering from her broken leg, and they need a room that is wheelchair accessible."

"Oh, Avie." Juliette turned to Tristan. "She's the niece that's—"

"Four. I remember you talking about her."

Mathilde gave him a frown and said, "She's a little firecracker. I think you'll like her. And once she gets comfortable with people, she'll be asking for them all the time. I'm sure she'll do the same with you."

He tried not to smile as he saw Juliette gulp, but the corner of his lips rose, breaking through all resistance. She looked at him with the same look she'd had after receiving the phone call from her mother the day before. The color drained from her face, and she closed her eyes for a moment, causing him to choke back a smile.

"Of course. I'd like that." He smiled at Mathilde, and the woman's face showed such relief that what had started out as a forced smile turned into a genuine one.

Juliette walked up the stairs, and he followed, surprised by the tightness of it. He had to turn sideways to make sure the bags got through as one wheel got stuck between the balusters. When they finally made it to the landing of the first floor, he was grateful, drawing in breaths as though he hadn't breathed in minutes.

Juliette walked straight to one of the doors and opened it. "This is where you'll stay. As you can see, my oldest brother, Henri, was really into rock bands."

Taking a step through the door, Tristan noted the large posters hung around the room, hiding all the walls behind them. He chuckled and said, "He didn't want to take all these with him when he got married?"

With a light laugh, Juliette said, "No, his wife put a stop to that. My family doesn't get many overnight visitors outside of the family, so I guess my mother hasn't felt the need to change anything."

She moved to grab her luggage, and Tristan shook his head, keeping his hand wrapped around the handle. Her frown made him laugh. Turning to move out of the room, Tristan waited for her to go in front of him as he carried the suitcase up one more flight of steep stairs.

"Your room is on the second floor? An elevator would've been nice."

She tipped her head back and laughed, causing him to smile. "You have no idea how many times I've thought that over the years. My parents' room is on the first floor, along with my brothers' rooms. My sister and I were upstairs while growing up, and even when the boys were at university or got married and moved away, my mother didn't want to move the stuff they'd left behind. Now I feel like my legs are on fire."

His eyes dipped to her calves a few steps above him, and he couldn't help but admire the definition to them. One of the bags slammed into the wall as they turned once more, and he shook his head, telling himself to focus on moving up the stairs. This was a business contract, and that's all he needed to worry about. He just wished he could feel what his brain was telling him instead of his heart going rogue with feelings of attraction and admiration.

Once they made it to the landing of the second floor, he paused for a moment, trying to catch his breath. Juliette placed her hands on her hips, her chest expanding and contracting as much as his.

Looking around the room, he saw a small sitting room, the far wall lined with books. Two closed doors sat on either side. Juliette stopped in front of one, looking as though an internal debate were going on in her head.

"Okay, just know that my mother hates change, so it probably still looks like it did when I graduated from school." Her eyes were pleading with him, and he gave her a small smile before nodding.

She took a deep breath and opened the door, looking at the floor as he moved past her. Setting the bag on the bed, he looked around, surprised to find several posters of music bands he recognized from when he was in high school. He smiled as he saw what must have been some of her favorites because of the hearts around the heads of the band members.

"It looks like you had your own music obsessions."

A bright pink tinged her cheeks, and he couldn't help but grin at her. "Yes, well, music meant a lot to me at the time. I kind of lived vicariously through the songs, and it was an escape, before I was able to move to Paris, that is."

Tristan glanced around the room, and what captured his attention most was a canvas of the sunset, the sky painted with several colors, and a young girl standing on a cliff admiring it. Juliette must have painted it as an early teen because it wasn't quite the caliber he could imagine for an adult with several years of artistic ability, but it evoked such emotion in him, like a freedom the girl was looking for.

He walked forward and stood in front of it. "This is amazing. Did you paint it?"

She nodded. "It was a project for one of my classes in school. I had to portray something in one of the books we were reading, and that's what I pictured. I've always liked it, even though I can't remember the book we discussed."

"Is this a real place?" He pointed to it and studied her face.

Shaking her head, she said, "No, just something I came up with. High school was really hard for me because…well, let's just say I'm glad to leave all those memories behind."

Tristan stepped forward and took her hand, which shot a jolt through him.

Juliette looked down at their hands and then up to him, a vulnerability in her eyes. Whatever she'd been through, it looked as though it still haunted her.

He closed the distance between them and wrapped his arms around her.

Several moments went by where they just stood there, Juliette's head resting on his shoulder. He hadn't held a girl in a long time, but it seemed to comfort both of them, helping him to relax a bit more. Maybe this trip would seal the wounds he'd felt for over a decade.

Pulling back, he looked into her eyes and then down to her lips. She didn't move, and he hesitated before moving forward.

A voice sounded from the floor below. "We'll be eating in thirty minutes!" It was Mathilde. Perfect timing.

Juliette stepped back and glanced down at her suitcase, unzipping it. She pulled out a few shirts and avoided his gaze.

"Do you still paint or draw?"

Her lips turned down, and she shook her head. "No, not since drawing the design for my business logo. With all of the research, marketing, and meeting with manufacturers and other business owners, I don't get a lot of downtime."

"I bet you'd be amazing at it. But I get it. That sounds a lot like my life the past few years."

"What hobby would you have if you had time for one?" Juliette had her hands clasped behind her back, and she twisted back and forth a bit while she waited for his answer.

Tristan took a minute to think about it and said, "It sounds odd, but probably horseback riding. I used to go a lot as a kid, but then when we moved to Paris from one of the suburbs, it was harder and harder to fit it in. It was always something I loved, though."

"I thought you said it was something you couldn't do. Like when we were talking about jousting?"

"I don't think I could trust myself to stay atop the horse while holding on to a long pole. Not long enough to make it a contest. It's been so long that I've forgotten most of the techniques."

Juliette grinned as she studied his face a bit more. Something broke her gaze away because she glanced down at the bag on the bed. Tristan saw the hint of pink at the tips of her ears and wondered what she was thinking.

"After we get unpacked, I'll show you around." She bit her lip as she thought about it, drawing his attention to her mouth. Her lips looked so soft, and with every touch from her soft hands, he knew the creams and oils she created must be contributing to that.

He felt drawn to her even more, and the smell of her perfume seemed to put him in a trance, the floral scent matching her cheery personality.

Juliette looked up at him as though she'd asked a question.

"I'm sorry. Did you ask me something?"

She grinned and said, "Go down and unpack. I'll come get you when I'm done."

Tristan took a seat on the edge of the bed, surprised at the stiffness of it.

He wasn't sure if she'd seen his expression but she said, "To be honest, neither bed will be all that comfortable, so I hope you can get some sleep while you're here."

Tristan looked at her, confused. "But your mom said they bought them last year."

Juliette closed her eyes and sat on the bed, the mattress bouncing her more like a board than the softness he was used to at home. "They buy them from a different store than you do. And the ones that are harder are usually cheaper." She shrugged and went to unpack her stuff, placing the clothes in small piles on the rack of wooden shelves.

Tristan nodded. "I'll be fine." He hesitated and turned to look at her. "Are there any rules you want to put into place for our situation?"

She stopped and sat on the bed again, looking up at him with those sea-blue eyes. "That's a good question." Pausing for a moment, she finally said, "Just don't fall in love with me." Her chuckle afterward seemed to rattle around in Tristan's chest, and he laughed as well.

"I think we'll be good on that. We'll be good friends who will work together on building your company to spread internationally." He gave her a close-lipped smile, trying to convince himself it was the truth. But there were so many conflicting emotions within him, and he wasn't quite sure what to do about it. He just needed to focus on the prize.

Juliette shrugged her shoulders and said, "I think we'll be okay. Just go along with the public displays of affection around my family, and if anyone comes by, for my parents' friends. Other than that, just do what you need to do to make it through these next two weeks."

"Sounds good. I'll leave you to unpack." Tristan stood and moved to the door. He looked back, and she gave him a shy smile, the color reaching her ears this time.

Moving down the narrow staircase, her words were on repeat in his mind. "Just don't fall in love with me." What would make her so worried about that? Then again, with all of the electricity between them, he'd have to take better precautions to guard his heart, or he might just lose it all over again.

CHAPTER 14

After everything was unpacked, Juliette showed Tristan where the bathroom was, tucked between two rooms down the hall. At least there was one upstairs. He couldn't imagine having to go down and then back up those stairs in the middle of the night.

"Your parents must be in good shape to come up here all the time." They stood next to the stairs, Tristan's hand resting on the newel post.

"I thought so too until my mom called about six weeks ago and said my dad had a heart attack. It was pretty scary, but at least he's doing okay now." Her face showed slight worry as they began their descent, but she hid it well. The mask of a slight smile could've easily fooled him.

Trying to decide if he wanted to ask the question, Tristan finally said out loud, "Did you come home to see him then?"

Juliette nodded. "Yeah, but I only stayed one night here, as the rest of the time we were at the hospital an hour away. Isabelle flew in for the weekend and headed back once my father had stabilized. My parents aren't that old, but now that all these health problems are surfacing, I need to come out more often. But with work, that can get tricky."

He made it to the ground floor, feeling as if he'd just gotten a short workout in. How was it that taking the steep stairs down could fuel the burn in his quads more than when he went up them?

Juliette stopped at the bottom of the stairs and looked at him. "What about your parents? Are you close to them? Do they live nearby?"

"They live a few blocks from my house, but they've been traveling for most of this year. They still call and talk to me about once a week, no matter where they are."

Juliette nodded and turned, walking toward the dimly lit family room. She moved to stand over one of the recliners. Tristan wasn't sure what she was doing at first, but when he moved behind her, he saw an older man lying in the chair.

"Papa. I'm home." The man's eyes fluttered for a minute and then finally opened, a broad smile crossing his face.

"Oh, my girl. I'm glad you're here." His breathing increased with each sentence he said, and Tristan wondered if there was something worse with his health than just a heart attack.

She leaned in to kiss both cheeks and then gave him a hug, and the two of them embraced for what seemed like minutes. As close as Tristan was with his parents, they didn't hug or show much affection. Maybe that was why he always tried to go above and beyond to be successful, hoping to hear the little phrases his dad gave him to show he was proud.

"Come sit down. And who is this you've brought with you?" The man grinned again, and Tristan moved forward, sticking his hand out.

"I'm Tristan, Juliette's boyfriend." It sounded a little off to his own ears, but he hadn't said the word boyfriend in connection to himself in eleven years. Eleven long years.

"Now, that's something I didn't think I'd hear in my lifetime. I'm Cyril Rousseau, and you've met Mathilde. Our Juliette here is the beautiful swan now."

Juliette put her hand on her father's and rolled her lips in with a panicked expression. "Now, Papa, we don't need to make Tristan feel uncomfortable, and the past is in the past. I'm happy now, and that's all that matters." She tried to smile, but it didn't reach her eyes, making Tristan more curious about what happened in her life to make her past so painful.

"Has she shown you some of her art?" her father asked him.

"Only what is on display in her room," Tristan said with a mischievous grin.

Cyril patted his daughter's hand and beamed at her. A few seconds later, his expression fell, and he looked as though he might cry. "I'm sorry I made you come back here, my cygne."

Why did he keep calling her his swan? What was Tristan missing?

Juliette smiled, but even though they'd only known each other a few days, Tristan had already begun to distinguish her genuine smile from the one she used to put on a brave face.

"I'm fine, Papa. I'll get to work on the dishes tomorrow, and we'll get everything ready. We still have time to get a lot done."

"But the throwing and the drying and the firing. Not to mention the glazing. Are you sure you can do it all by yourself?"

Juliette reached forward and touched her father's cheek. "Of course, Papa. You taught me how to do it."

Tristan was surprised by the love he saw between the two of them. With her mother, Juliette had seemed somewhat short. The only explanation he could think of was that she and her father had spent long hours together crafting and creating the pieces they sold. If Tristan found someone to love, he'd want to show it as much as possible. And he had, once.

"Where is Maman? I didn't see her in the kitchen."

Cyril closed his lips as if trying not to give away a big secret. "She went into town to buy a few more things for dinner."

"Whatever she's cooking smells really good." Tristan grinned at Cyril who agreed. His taste buds were more excited about it than he'd realized. Maybe if he'd learned to cook a little over the years, he wouldn't still be burning the easier prepackaged foods Angela had stocked in his home.

"Mathilde is one of the best cooks in Brittany. She can whip up something out of almost nothing, and she has a few times, especially when times were slim. I don't know what I would do without that woman." The man smiled and took in a breath, looking more tired than when they'd first woken him up.

Juliette patted his hand and pulled up a blanket over his upper body. "Rest, Papa. We'll catch up more later."

Before she moved away, he said, "Best to go change into something for company, my dear. It seems as though your mother's invited the town for a welcome home party for you."

Tristan watched as panic shot over Juliette's face and she stood straight as a board, not for the first time that day. He reached forward, placing his hand on the small of her back, and was surprised when she leaned into it a bit. He draped an arm around her shoulders and put his mouth next to her ear. "Don't worry. I'm here. Let's go change, and we'll figure this out."

What had happened in this town to make her so nervous in front of people? In Paris, she'd been confident and hadn't shied away from speaking her mind to him. What was it that made her want to draw into herself?

She nodded to her father with a stony expression. Against his open palm, she felt like dead weight for a moment before she took steps forward, looking as if her legs were made of wood. Once she got to the stairs, she became lifelike again and ran up them, skipping several on her way up. Tristan did his best to catch up but was surprised at how fast she moved.

Finding her sobbing in a heap on her bed, Tristan froze at the door. What was he supposed to do in this situation? He'd seen girls cry before, but he'd never had to be the one to comfort them. Camila had only cried in front of him once, and that had been something much less complicated than the situation he now found himself in.

Moving forward, he sat next to her on the bed, pulling her hair away from her face and laying it on the bed behind her. Large droplets dripped down her nose and cheeks as her body shook from the sobs. Taking his fingers, he combed through her hair, only going out a few inches before beginning again at the scalp. He remembered how much it had soothed him as a boy when something troubled him.

A minute or two later, the tears dried up, and she stared at the wall across from her.

"Are you okay? Do you want to talk about something?" he said, trying to keep his voice low. He wondered if she'd fallen asleep as her breathing had evened out and her eyes were still closed. If this was how girls acted, maybe it was better for him to stay away.

She finally opened her eyes and sat up, moving to rest her back against the wall. Pulling her legs up, she put her hands over her face, her long hair cascading down and covering everything.

Throwing back her hair, she said, "I'm so sorry about that. I feel like an idiot now. I promise I don't act like I'm seven all the time. Just when my mother does things she knows I'm not comfortable with."

Reaching out his arm, he pulled her head to lean on his shoulder. "I can understand that. What makes you scared of a party?"

She gave him a look like he had ten heads, and he fought back a smile. "I know it might seem odd for an attractive guy like yourself to imagine, but some of us aren't the best at being the center of attention. Especially here in Dinan."

"Okay, I feel like there's a big secret you aren't telling me. If I'm going to get us through this surprise party without blowing our cover, I think I need to know what it is."

"Promise you won't give me pity looks or anything?"

Tristan twisted his mouth to the side. "Uh, sure."

"I had really bad acne in high school, to the point that it looked like an experiment for a biology class. I grew my hair out really long and was able to hide it for the most part, except for our outdoor fitness classes where I had to pull it into a ponytail. I was called everything in the book for years and several times wanted to just hide out at home."

That was the reason. "That's why you started your company, to find a solution for your problems."

Juliette nodded. "I'd tried for a few years but hadn't found anything that worked long-term. The few months before graduation, I tried another mixture and was surprised to find that within a few days, my skin had cleared of all the red splotches and welts, revealing regular skin. But of course, kids can be cruel and wouldn't forget how

I'd looked before." She looked down at the floor and pulled her lips in, looking rejected.

Tristan tipped her head back until she looked at him. "Have you looked in the mirror lately? Because you're beautiful." His fingers trailed down the side of her face as his eyes moved to her lips. The urge to kiss her was growing with every second they stared at one another.

She finally pulled away, her eyes inspecting her fingernails. "Thank you." It was a soft whisper, and he almost didn't catch it.

Hopping up, Tristan said, "Okay, so what can we do to make you feel better? Is there an outfit or blouse that makes you feel confident? I usually wear a suit, so I'm not as knowledgeable about what you women like."

Juliette looked at him, her eyebrows furrowed. "This might be more experience than you expected for advertising to women, Tristan." She smiled at him, and it seemed to do a lap around his heart. After a moment, she scooted off the bed and pulled out one of the shirts on the bottom of the pile. It was a blueish-colored short-sleeved blouse.

"Do you wear a skirt with that? Shorts?" He really was rusty when it came to women's clothing. He'd been designing campaigns for men's stuff for so long and hadn't had a girlfriend in longer that he was lost as to what they needed.

She pulled out another folded item, a darker gray material. He wondered why she was staring at him and then he realized. "Sorry, I'll just wait for you in the room out there."

He closed the door and walked over to the row of books, selecting one from the shelf. Thumbing through it, he was surprised when less than a minute later, the door opened and Juliette came out. Working to keep his jaw from dropping to the floor, he smiled at her.

"You look amazing." The blouse accentuated the color of her eyes, and the trim of the gray skirt showed off her curves just enough that Tristan gulped and moved his eyes higher.

He walked over and placed his hands on her upper arms, ducking his head a little to see into her eyes. "How do you feel?"

She smiled, the action lighting up her face more than he'd seen since they'd left Paris. "Better. Thank you."

"Are you ready to go downstairs?" he asked, tucking a piece of hair behind her ear.

She shivered, and he wondered if she was cold. It seemed as though she did that a lot, even though he thought he might die of heat exposure.

She nodded and said, "Ready."

Tristan stuck out his arm, and she slipped hers through it as the two of them walked down the stairs of a future broken ankle slowly. When they got to the bottom, things were still quiet.

"They'll be waiting outside for us." Her head turned toward the living room, and she searched in the dim light. "Papa is gone from the recliner, and I didn't hear them upstairs."

Turning her to him, Tristan said, "Just be the girl you are in Paris. Confident, smart, witty, and always beautiful, even if she forgets her metro card." He winked at her, happy to see red tingeing her cheeks.

Her eyes moved to his lips, and Tristan leaned in an inch before remembering this was a fake relationship. He'd probably have to kiss her in the near future, but there was no one to impress at that moment.

Opening the door, he waved her through, hoping he'd know how to help her through this.

CHAPTER 15

$\mathcal{A}$s much as she was shaking, Juliette was grateful for the calm manner Tristan had taken with her over the past half-hour. Days ago, she wouldn't have imagined he'd be so sweet and patient. But at least she'd told him what had happened and he hadn't run away. Then again, he hadn't seen pictures of her from back then, and she hoped he never would.

She'd glanced at his lips, wondering what they would feel like on hers. As much as she was telling herself she couldn't fall for this guy, it seemed her insides weren't responding to those commands. He'd leaned in a bit, and she'd felt a nervous suspense at the thought of him kissing her. What was worse was the disappointment she felt when he stepped back and opened the door for her.

He was her fake boyfriend. What did she expect when there was no one to convince around them?

Walking through the door, she jumped as several people shouted, "Surprise!" Besides the Fête des Remparts, her family only celebrated birthdays and Christmas, so to have a party planned for her home-coming, Juliette couldn't see what her mom was thinking when she'd put it together.

"We're so happy to see you back, Juliette," said Coline Viceny, one of their neighbors. "Your parents talk about you and your business all the time. I like to tell my friends I was one of your first customers."

Laughing, Juliette kissed both cheeks of the older woman and stood back. "Yes, you did. I remember the first cream didn't work out so well, and you ended up with blisters. I'm so glad we finally found something that worked for you."

This was good for her, the small talk and the reminiscing about the good things in her life.

Coline took her hand. "You look like you're on a cloud, my dear. I hope you've been able to find happiness." She looked behind Juliette. "And who might this attractive tall drink of water be?" She was over sixty years old, but the woman always claimed she was a twenty-year-old trapped in an old woman's body.

Turning to Tristan, Juliette said, "This is Tristan."

The woman stepped forward, kissing each cheek before stepping back, her eyebrow raised. "Boyfriend?"

Juliette hesitated before nodding, and Tristan said, "Yes, ma'am. We've been dating three, no, four months now?" He turned his head to look at Juliette for confirmation, and she just about fainted, knowing that any man who asked her opinion would make her a happy woman.

Coline looked at Juliette and winked. "Looks like he's a keeper."

She moved away, and several others came up to talk to them. With Tristan's arm around her shoulders, she felt the confidence she'd left in Paris start to come back. All of the people who'd come were friends of her parents and had been the ones to help her get a start in selling her products. As she saw each one of them, she realized how much their kindness during some of the darkest times in her life had helped shape her now.

Her mother stood and said, "We just wanted to thank everyone for coming out today. It's been a while since we've had our girl here, and we're so grateful she came out to help us get ready for the festival. You're amazing, Juliette, and we're so proud of all you've been able to accomplish over the last few years."

Juliette's cheeks heated, and she nodded, hoping everyone would stop staring at her. All she had to do was get through the next few hours, and then she could relax.

* * *

Two hours later, Juliette sat in a chair, her brain mentally exhausted from talking to so many people. Only about fifteen or so people remained, all the ones closest to her parents. They'd talked about the heart attack and how her father had collapsed at the grocery store. After that, someone had brought up Juliette's skin care company. She was grateful the topics hadn't turned to what a recluse she'd been for a while. That was all she needed for Tristan to think she was loony.

With her head down, she saw someone approach from the side, and at first, she thought it was Tristan. Looking up, she saw the bald man was shorter by at least six inches. Taking a few seconds to look closer, she said, "Timmy?"

"Yep. It's me." He stuffed his hands in his pockets and looked uncomfortable, glancing around everywhere but at Juliette's face.

A moment of panic welled up inside her as his face called up the memory of a party she'd been invited to, and all she could see were the fireworks going off right in front of her, burning her. Timmy had been her closest friend throughout most of her school years, but she could still see his smiling face as the car raced away from her home with a few other teens.

Doing her best to compose herself, she asked, "Do you live around here? I haven't heard how you've been over the last few years."

She wasn't sure she really wanted to know, but she knew it was the polite thing to ask. Forgiveness had taken her a while when it came to him, but now, seeing him, she was grateful she had. It appeared as if the past ten years had not been kind to him, and even though he'd betrayed her, she hated to think that he'd suffered so much since the days when they'd been studying for final exams.

"I still live at home. I lost my job when I got into a car accident, and I take odd jobs here and there that I can do." He paused a moment, running one of his hands over the top of his head. "I just wanted to…I felt bad for—"

"Hey, *mon coeur*. Do you need anything from inside?" Tristan asked, leaning over her shoulder.

Had he just called her "love"? She put a hand over her chest to hide her heart trying to break through it.

"I think I'm good for now, thank you, *mon amour*." She tried to keep her face neutral, like it was a common occurrence to call a guy that looked like he could be French royalty something sweet.

The corners of his mouth ticked up, and he looked over at Tim, stretching out his hand as he had so often that day. "Hi there, I'm Tristan."

"Tim."

"What is it you came to tell my girl?"

Tim opened and closed his mouth several times, the sound getting caught in his throat. "I just came to tell her how sorry I was for how I treated her a while back. I'm glad to see your face healed well, from the acne and the, uh, fire." He shifted onto one foot, staring at the ground for a few seconds before turning his gaze back to Juliette. "I see now that I was in the wrong, that I should've stuck by your side and been the friend you needed me to be."

Clearing the mound that had formed in her throat, she nodded and said, "That was a long time ago, Timmy. I've moved on. But I appreciate the apology."

He nodded and turned to leave, the limp in his gait making Juliette feel bad for him.

Tristan sat next to her, and she leaned her head on his shoulder as if it were the most natural thing in the world.

Tristan's words buzzed around in her mind, the word "love" echoing over and over again. She still couldn't believe how much her stomach went haywire when she was close to him. He'd been kind, gentle, and like a wall supporting her throughout the entire evening. She couldn't have picked a better fake boyfriend if she'd had options.

Sadness fell over her as she knew his words weren't real, making her long for a real connection, one not marred by a prize at the end.

He reached over and took her hand, intertwining his fingers with hers. The jolt of electricity shot through her, but the warmth of his hand calmed her nerves.

She looked up at him and laughed, reaching her free hand up to wipe at the different shades of lipstick. "It looks like you've made the rounds and met most of the women here." She grinned and he nodded.

"I got a lot of requests for two kisses on each side, saying that's what you do here in Dinan to greet each other."

Juliette's mouth dropped open and she laughed. "I'm sure they took advantage of your good looks. Thanks again for being here." She looked down at their intertwined hands and smiled.

"So, Timmy, huh?" Tristan's voice was low and Juliette almost didn't catch it.

"Yeah," she said, eyes closed, just savoring the moment with her hand in his. People still chatted around them, her parents loving a reason to invite neighbors over. She was just grateful she didn't need to make small talk for a few minutes.

"What did he do?"

Juliette bit her bottom lip and looked up at his molten eyes. "I'm not sure you want to know."

"After everything I've seen and heard over the past two days, I think knowing would be better for me as your fake boyfriend."

"Promise you won't go beat him up?" Juliette knew she shouldn't be joking about it, but she found she couldn't stop herself from smirking.

Tristan rolled his eyes. "Promise. He said something about fire. What happened?"

Juliette lifted her head and looked at him. "Timmy and I weren't the most popular people in school. When we got invited to a party to celebrate the end of the year, I was waiting for him to pick me up. But when I opened the door to go outside, there were several lit fireworks going off right next to me." Motioning to her chin, she lifted it a bit to show him. "I have a scar here from one of the sparks hitting me."

"I'm so sorry. I had no idea. Do you need me to knock some sense into him?" Tristan looked in the direction Timmy had gone.

Resting her head back on Tristan's shoulder, she said, "No, I think he feels bad enough as it is. Let's just sit here for a few more minutes."

Tristan wrapped an arm around her, pulling her even closer to him and combing his fingers through her hair. She didn't know what magic his fingers held, but when he did that, it seemed as if the world was falling away.

"Was it all a joke, then?"

Juliette couldn't hold back the tears any longer as she nodded.

He kissed the top of her head as he pulled her closer, and she was unsure but thought she heard him whisper under his breath, "I'm broken too."

She wasn't sure what he meant by that, but with all the help he'd given her over just the past eight hours, she hoped he would trust her enough to talk about it soon enough. If she could help him through something the way he was for her, she'd do it in a heartbeat.

CHAPTER 16

*S*o, you're the one dating my granddaughter, huh?"

Tristan turned to find an older gentleman sitting to his right.

Juliette sat up and grinned. "Grandpa. How are you?" She leaned over Tristan to hug her grandpa, and her perfume floated up to him again, making his insides flip. What was going on with him?

Juliette moved back, and Tristan looked at the man and answered his question with a, "Yes, sir."

"This is my grandpa, Robert Pascal. He lives upstairs in one of the boys' old rooms."

"It's a pleasure to meet you, sir. What have you been up to today?" Tristan remembered Juliette saying he lived there, but he hadn't seen him once throughout the several hours since they'd arrived.

A mischievous smile crossed Robert's face. "Son, when you get to be old like me, you can be cranky, say what you want, and sleep as long as you like. Napping is a new pastime." A laugh escaped his lips, and Tristan couldn't help but join in. Since all of his grandparents had passed a long time ago, he didn't have the opportunity to interact with many people Robert's age. It was more fun than he'd expected.

Several other people took up seats around them, chatting here and there. Tristan saw the tiredness on Juliette's face, and he felt the same, wishing he could crash on the bed upstairs and sleep until the next morning. He was used to working hard at his job, but it seemed that with all of the emotional ups and downs of the day, he was more tired than he'd been in quite a while.

"I heard you two have been dating for some time." The woman spoke from a few chairs away. He remembered being introduced to her at the beginning of the party, but with so many names in between, he couldn't put a finger on hers.

"Yes." He felt Juliette tighten a little in his arms and wondered what had caused it. He glanced around but didn't see anything significant.

The woman looked at Juliette and asked, "How is it, kissing a billionaire?"

Tristan's insides froze, and now he understood why Juliette reacted that way so often. He was used to bluntness, but this was taking it to a whole other level.

"I just looked you up," she said, waving her phone at them. "It seems you've had a pretty successful career, taking over your father's business and making boatloads in return. So, Juliette, does all that money make kissing him that much sweeter?"

Juliette opened her mouth to say something and then turned to him, her sapphire eyes pulling him in, making him want to kiss her. Just so she'd be able to say something, of course.

"Just like kissing anyone else, I'm sure." Juliette's tone was dry, and Tristan was ready to send this woman packing.

"You're sure? You don't know?" The woman's lips were pinched together, as if accusing them of some mistake.

Juliette's voice wouldn't come out, and Tristan finally said, "She means that it's just like any kiss. I don't get extra points on the kissing front for what's in my bank account." The edge to his voice came out harder than he'd intended, but the woman clamped her mouth shut and sat back, so it had the intended results.

"Billionaire? What? Tristan, you're a billionaire?" Mathilde walked over and stood before him and Juliette, eyes narrowed. "You didn't tell me that."

"Would that have mattered, Maman? We've never been ones to worry about how much money a person has. I don't know why you're so worried about it, Sasha. Just because the media portrays him as a bad boy doesn't mean it's true. He's been a true gentleman with me." She turned to look at him, giving him a small smile.

Her words hit home in his chest, and he'd never been so grateful for someone standing up for him. Was that what she really thought? Or was that something she said because of their arrangement? From the look on her face, he would say that was how she really felt.

A hand waved in the air next to them, and Robert said, "Why don't you kiss now so Sasha can be satisfied?"

Both of their heads snapped to look at him, and Tristan wasn't sure what to do. Another situation where they should've discussed the rules beforehand. He was fine kissing Juliette, but would she be okay with an audience like this?

"I haven't seen the two of you so much as give each other a peck since you got here." Mathilde's voice turned sing-song at the end, and he wondered what he should do.

When the others in the group started chanting, "Kiss! Kiss!" like they were back in grade school, Tristan knew there was only one way to get them to stop.

Turning toward Juliette, he was ready to kiss her, even with the awkward tension around them, but she surprised him by standing.

"I'm not kissing someone, my boyfriend even, just because you don't have the opportunity to kiss someone as amazing as Tristan. Go find someone who will put up with your sarcasm." With that, she turned and marched off around the side of the house.

It only took a few moments for Tristan to register what had happened before he was on his feet and moving after her. Once he caught up to her, she was leaning on the other side of the house, the shade making the space cool.

With her jaw clenched and fists curled into a ball, he tried to hide a smile as he saw the spark of the girl he'd met in Paris.

"Are you all right?" he asked softly.

She nodded and blew out a breath. "Yeah."

"Do you want to talk about it?"

"Is it wrong that saying that felt really good? There's something about this place that makes me revert back to the person I was when I lived here, but telling Sasha exactly what I was thinking was something I've dreamed of doing for longer than I want to admit." She giggled, and Tristan smiled, grateful she was okay with it.

Placing his hands on her arms, he said, "I'm glad you did that. She was out of line to demand such a thing."

Juliette ran a hand through her hair and looked up at the darkening sky. "I'll probably get an earful from my mother later, but I just need to remember who I am when I'm in Paris. That's the real me, and I don't have to be goaded into doing things I don't want to do."

Tristan tried to keep a straight face as he said, "Like bringing along a fake boyfriend."

She rested her head back against the rock of the house and sighed. "Okay, well, I guess I'll get there eventually. At least this is a breakthrough, right?"

"I'd say so. I like this side of you a lot better." Tristan wrapped his arms around her, pulling her into him. He liked that she fit so well against him, her head resting on his shoulder. It was something small, but he didn't want to let go, at least not yet.

CHAPTER 17

The next morning, looking out the window, the sun was higher than he'd seen it in weeks upon waking, causing him to panic. He hated to be the late sleeper, preferring to be up and getting an early start on the day. What would her parents think of him sleeping this late?

After scrambling to get the bed made, he ran up to Juliette's room and found her still asleep as well. Looking at his phone, he realized it was only seven in the morning. Not wanting to mess up the bed he'd already made nor go back down those stairs half-awake, he dropped onto the floor next to her.

When he woke again, he noticed the bed was empty, and Juliette was creeping around him, trying to put something back on the shelf to his side.

"I'm awake," he said, running a hand over his face. Clicking on his phone, he saw it was eight thirty.

"Did you not sleep well?" she asked, sitting on the edge of the bed.

Tristan smiled at her through heavily-lidded eyes. "I mean, it wasn't my bed at home, but with the late night last night, I think I was pretty dead. I woke up earlier this morning, thinking it was a lot later than it was and had already made the bed." He looked down to see a blanket covering him. The thoughtfulness of the act warmed him.

"I wanted to thank you for everything you did yesterday. Honestly, you went above and beyond, and I couldn't be more grateful." The look on her face was tender, as if she were holding back several emotions.

Giving her a crooked smile, he said, "No problem. I'm just happy it worked out."

"I never would have guessed my mother would be so happy for me telling Sasha off. She's never been that proud of me, not that I can remember anyway."

She was close enough that he could lean up and kiss her. But would she want that? She was treating this as the original agreement, fake boyfriend for a contract. Maybe she didn't want more than that. What if he'd been the only one to feel anything from their hand-holding and hugs?

"Are you getting up? I have to get started in the shop this morning. I'd love to show it to you if you're interested. I never got a chance to give you the full tour last night." She cocked her head to the side and gave him a small smile. Those little looks were shooting holes in the wall he'd built around his heart.

Throwing off the blanket, he said, "I'm up. Just give me a minute or two to change." He looked over to find her in clothes that looked worn and had several spots across them. "I take it you're planning on getting dirty today."

"Yeah, I've got to see what we have already made and make a plan for how to get things done before the festival. I can see if you can borrow a shirt from my father if you want."

With a nod, Tristan said, "That would be great. I may as well help out if I can while I'm here." He winced at the words. It made it seem as though he was ready to go home as soon as possible. While he missed his expensive bed, he felt more at ease here than he had in a long time.

Juliette left the room, and Tristan followed until the next floor down, where he slipped into his room to change. He pulled on some jeans, knowing they would probably get ruined, but as they weren't his favorite, he didn't mind as much.

He pulled off his shirt just as Juliette walked into the room. Her eyes went wide, and her jaw dropped an inch, just enough to tell him she was embarrassed.

"Sorry, I should have knocked." She turned quickly and threw him the shirt before walking out. He didn't wait long to follow, emerging with the spotted green shirt on. He did all he could to keep the smile from his face, having to bite the side of his cheek to keep it neutral.

After tying his sneakers, he touched her on the shoulder. "Are you ready?" he asked, a huge smile plastered across his face.

"Yes, yes I am." She trotted down the steps, and Tristan followed, making it to the ground floor easier than the day before.

Mathilde walked in through the door with a basket in her hand, placing it on the kitchen table. "Help yourself. Fresh croissants and a nice warm baguette."

"Thanks, Maman." Juliette reached in and pulled out a croissant, while Tristan tore off a piece of the baguette. Mathilde set a jar of jam on the table and he spread some across the bread.

"We'll take this out into the studio, Maman. Thank you for these." Juliette raised her croissant and smiled.

"Working already this morning? Make sure to save some time for lunch." Her words floated out to them as they walked out the door.

Juliette led him around the corner of the house, opening a door to what looked like an addition.

"This is the shop," she said, motioning to everything inside.

The space was neatly kept and held several tools Tristan didn't recognize. He hadn't grown up with much art around, except the paintings on the walls of his childhood home, and he was surprised at how much space the tools took up. A wheel sat in the corner with what looked like a bucket of water next to it. A large stove was against the opposite wall, and in the middle of the room sat a long table, half of it covered with pieces of pottery and the other half with pieces of jewelry.

Tristan nodded. "Wow, this is incredible. This is where you spent a lot of time in high school, huh?"

"A lot more than I should have. Playing in the clay helped me think." Juliette smiled, and he tried to imagine what helped him do that. He usually just needed a tartelette aux frambois, and that helped him think really quickly.

"What do we need to do?"

Juliette pulled out a notepad and a pen, walking over to a large wall of shelves filled with several pieces of pottery. Tristan knew very little about it all, but it looked like these weren't yet finished.

Chewing on the tip of her pen, Juliette looked at him, finally registering what he'd said. "First off, I need to take inventory of what we have and at what stages everything is. Then I can make a plan for how to get it all done. Most of the pieces take at least a week to dry before they can be fired, meaning I need to get as many pieces thrown this week as I can to give them time to dry. In between, I'll have to work on jewelry and then go back to the firing and glazing of the pieces."

"How long does it take you to create one piece?"

She scrunched up her nose and bit on the end of the pen again, looking like she was trying to think it through. "I'm a little out of practice, so it might take me longer than I want it to. I used to be able to make fifteen plates in an hour, but I'll have to build back up to that."

He watched as she began counting the pieces on the wall, her lips moving ever so slightly. It would be better if he could focus on something other than her lips all the time. The desire to kiss her was growing stronger and stronger, and he couldn't get it out of his mind, like telling himself he couldn't have dessert but being unable to get it out of his head for the next week.

"Can I help you count things?"

Juliette laughed, throwing open a door he hadn't seen. "Sure. We'll need to count each plate, bowl, larger bowl, pitcher, etc. Just shout out what it is and how many so I can write it down. I'll come in there when I'm done out here."

They worked that way for close to thirty minutes, silence all around, except when Tristan shouted out what he'd counted and how many. Juliette joined him halfway through, having counted all the pieces waiting to be fired. All the pieces that had been fired but still needed the glaze and designs on them were in the large room where they were working, and Tristan was blown away by the quantity of things there.

"Do you think all this will be enough for the festival?"

Juliette bit one corner of her lip as she looked down at the paper. Shaking her head, she said, "I'm not sure. It's been a while since I've done a festival, and I'll have to check my dad's notes. My initial reaction is no, but it would be nice to only need to throw a few pieces and glaze the rest."

She pulled out a large ledger from under the large table in the other room, and Tristan was surprised by the detail the notes contained. "Your parents keep all of this information in a book? That's a lot to know. If they had it on a spreadsheet, they'd be able to analyze it better, tell what they've been selling more of and what the demand is, depending on the year, right?"

Juliette nodded. "Yeah, you're right. I've never really thought of doing it another way, just because this is how my parents always ran it. But if we could get these notes into a spreadsheet and then teach them how to use it, it might come in handy for future festivals and other sales." She gave him a side-eye and a small smirk.

"Would you like me to do all that?" Tristan asked, catching on to her hint.

"Would you? That would be amazing." Her look was innocent, like she hadn't thought of that, even though her quick response told him that was exactly what she wanted him to do. "You can work at the big table while I throw some bowls. It looks like we're really short on those, especially for people who want sets." She paused for a moment and then said, "Do you want to learn how to create something out of clay first before grabbing your computer?"

"Yeah, I'm ready to watch the master work." He grinned at her, and she rolled her eyes, a huge grin taking over her face while her cheeks turned a blush color.

She waved him over to the wheel and sat down. "Okay, we clean off the wheel really well after we're done. But then we always check to make sure it's clean when we're going to start another project. The clay goes in the middle of the wheel." She grabbed a block of clay from a container on a shelf and placed it onto the wheel. With her thumb, she pushed down small sections around the bottom of the clay.

"I'm assuming that is to secure it to the wheel?" Tristan asked, looking over her shoulder. He was mesmerized as her fingers knew exactly what they needed to do.

She nodded and continued pushing.

As she pointed to the floor, he saw her foot sitting on a pedal.

"This helps to turn the wheel as fast or as slow as you want. When you just begin, the best thing to do is go slow so you can get a feel for the clay and learn which way to go with it. The most important thing is to get the clay well-centered, which we do through a process called coning up and coning down, like this."

He watched as she moved her hands into an A shape, putting them around the clay and forming it in her hands.

She stopped and looked up at him. "Do you want to try?"

Part of him wanted to, but he knew she had a lot of work to do as it was. "Are you sure we have the time?"

The side of her mouth turned up as she looked at him. "We'll be fine. Come sit here, and we'll work on it."

Juliette stood and had him sit down, helping him form his hands over the clay. She tried several times, but he kept switching it at the wrong time. She shifted behind him, leaning over his shoulders and guiding his hands as he worked the clay.

"Okay, do you feel like the clay is moving from side to side, or does it feel centered and smooth?" Her lips were next to his ear, and the heat from her words sent a chill through his upper body.

He shook his head. "No, it seems to be centered to me." His words were just above a whisper. Clearing his throat, he said again, "At least, I think it is."

They worked through the clay, her hands helping guide his on the smooth surface, applying and releasing pressure every so often to show him the techniques. She let him go on his own for the last part, and by the end of the lesson, he'd made an uneven-shaped bowl.

"It looks really good." Juliette laughed and cut if off the wheel using a long piece of wire.

"Uh-huh, if you need a bowl with a section to sip your milk out of, this is it," Tristan said glumly as they washed their hands.

That started her laughing so much that she doubled over, working to catch her breath.

"Go ahead, laugh it up."

She reached out for his arm and said, "Tristan, you did a great job for your first time. Do you want to see what happened to my first cup?"

He nodded, curious.

It only took a minute or two for her to disappear into the other room and then reappear with a misshapen cup looking like it had folded in on itself.

Chuckling, Tristan pointed to it and asked, "That was your first throw?"

She raised her eyebrows as she nodded. "Does that make you feel better?"

"Maybe." He twisted his lips to the side and grinned.

"It's hard to believe, but there are a lot of things we have to mess up on before we can get better. Do you know how many tests we do for our products at Rousseau Belle? There are plenty of failures in life, but it's how you adjust and try again that shows the real value of a man."

Tristan opened his mouth to say something, but his brain kept replaying the words, only sped up. He'd always been taught that failure wasn't an option, that it was the mark of a weaker man. He'd done everything he could to avoid failure, but looking at it from her perspective, he found it easier to understand that it was okay for him to not be perfect.

"Thank you," he said. "I needed that."

She slid her arms around his waist to hug him, and that same feeling of them fitting together like puzzle pieces entered his mind. Now if he could just make it out of this fake relationship without getting any more attached. Because at this point, his heart was more in danger than it had been in over a decade.

CHAPTER 18

*J*uliette had spent much of the day throwing plates, ending it with a few pitchers. The one she'd had the hardest time with was the teapot, having difficulty getting the spout to form how she wanted it to. Being out of practice didn't help her any. Tristan kept her company most of the day and had gone through half of the ledger, entering it into a spreadsheet before they finished for the night.

Dinner was her mother's stew, and she was surprised at how much she'd missed it over the years. Nothing compared to the rich flavors and comfort she felt while eating it. She hadn't thought of memories being attached to a thing like stew, but she remembered several long talks she'd had with her parents over the years, often with a bowl of it in front of her.

When her phone rang after dinner and she saw Rachelle's name, she excused herself and walked outside, checking on some of the plants in the garden she paid her mother to take care of for Juliette's business. How grateful she was that even though she hadn't made the trip home in a long while, her parents still worked to help her with her business by growing the ingredients here on their property, harvesting them and sending them to her in Paris.

"Rachelle, how are things going there?"

"Things are running smoothly. We've had several new orders for that new cream, and the lip balm containers are on their way to us. We should have them ready to ship to retailers within the month."

Juliette blew out a breath, grateful that things hadn't imploded the minute she'd left. "Thanks for all your help with it. I won't be back until after the festival, so about three weeks. Do you think you can keep things under control until then?"

A sigh came from Rachelle's end before she said, "Of course. I'll make sure everything stays on track. How are things with Mr. Playboy?"

A smile crossed Juliette's face, and she couldn't help it. "He's really not how I always thought. He's kind and sweet, and such a gentleman. He helped me get through a panic session and then helped me get through a surprise party my mother threw me."

"That doesn't sound like something you'd love. Did it go okay?"

"One of the ladies started asking what it was like to kiss a billion-aire, and then they all chanted that we should kiss."

Rachelle must have been holding her breath, because Juliette didn't hear anything. Finally, she said, "And?"

"I told the lady off and walked away."

"No way! You didn't kiss him?"

Juliette sighed. "No, I didn't want to do anything in front of all those people. I've been tempted to lean in and kiss him a few times, and I think he's done the same. We just haven't kissed yet." She walked to the other side of the garden and said, "I don't know, Rachelle. I'm nearing the danger zone and don't know if I'll be okay when this is all over."

"Why does it have to be over? Obviously, he's feeling the sparks too. Maybe you can tame his heart." Rachelle giggled.

Juliette shook her head, using her foot to move some of the broken leaves. As much as she wanted to believe it, she knew she had to be realistic. "There is something in his past that he still hasn't shared with me. I'm hoping he'll trust me soon, but I think it could be the key as to why he's been a serial dater."

"Cereal hater?"

"No, serial dater, as in goes on lots of dates but never with the same woman."

"Oh!" Rachelle laughed. "I'm glad you clarified that. I was going to have to question if you were actually Juliette if you were judging him because he didn't like cereal." After a moment, she said, "Keep me updated. I want all the details."

Grateful for her friend's support—of what, she wasn't sure—she said, "Will do, Rachelle. Even though I shouldn't be falling for my fake boyfriend, I will let you know if any developments happen on the other side."

She hung up, picking at a few weeds around the plants as she tried to reel in her thoughts about the man in the house who was slowly stealing her heart.

CHAPTER 19

As the week passed, Tristan slowly built a website for the Rousseau family business. Each part was cleared by Mathilde, and she would pretend to critique things before acting excited about the whole process. Teaching them about receiving orders online had been an adventure, but he thought Juliette's father was slowly understanding.

Juliette worked from early in the morning until almost dinner day after day, throwing different pieces, and sometimes Tristan just stopped what he was doing, mesmerized by the precision of her hands as they moved through the clay. The skill and speed she had amazed him. The fact that she was able to create things of beauty as well as run a business made him feel the excitement of a kid on Christmas. He hadn't met someone as well-rounded who piqued his interest, and his curiosity made him want to learn all about her.

After four straight days of working day in and day out, he was surprised to see her dressed in shorts and a nicer top on Sunday morning.

"Are you not working in the studio today?"

She gave him a tired smile. "I could use a little break from it. I was thinking we could see some of the town. I wouldn't want you to come all the way out here and not see the beauty of Dinan."

Closing his laptop, Tristan stood. "I'm game for that. I needed something different today but wasn't sure what."

He followed her out the front door, and they started walking along the road that led into town.

Juliette pulled a piece of hair away from her face as she turned to Tristan. "How is it going, teaching my parents about technology?"

Blowing out an exaggerated breath, he said, "You weren't kidding when you said they struggle in that area. I think it took me almost two hours to teach them how to log in to the site."

"As long as the wifi doesn't disconnect, we won't have to worry about instructing them through that. Having them choose between all the options would be rough."

Tristan chuckled, sticking his hand in his pants pocket. "I'm surprised they even have wifi here."

"We're still on the edge of Dinan so it's not so remote that they can't have access to it. My parents wouldn't be happy if it went down because they use it for their 'shows.' I get a call about once a week to help them navigate to find the ones they want to watch. But they rotate through the four of us, so it happens almost every other day." The two of them laughed, and Tristan loved the sound of it.

They walked in silence for some time, Tristan taking in the beauty of the town. His initial reaction that it resembled an English town wasn't far off, as many of the houses boasted the similar timber front.

They walked to a large castle-like building, and Tristan said, "What is this?"

"The Chateau de Dinan. It was built in the late 1300s and is now used as a museum. There are some older artifacts throughout. They've also set up the upper floor to display paintings and other sculptures relating to the town."

They entered the building, and after watching Juliette craft with clay over the past few days, he wondered what it took to create the decorative trims surrounding the room. Every bit had to have taken so much time, and in a building this large, he could imagine it had taken a while to get it all finished.

They looked at a bunch of artifacts and older dishes, Tristan in awe of it all. This whole town was medieval in his eyes, from the festival coming up to the amount of older architecture and collections.

"So, did you have a girlfriend when you left for college?" Juliette kept her eyes forward toward a collection of pitchers, and from her glazed-over look, she'd seen them a few times.

Tristan took in a breath, trying to decide how much to tell her. They were fake dating after all. "Yeah, we started dating in high school. It lasted about a month after I went to the States. Then she married my best friend."

Juliette grimaced and reached over, touching his forearm. It sent a calming sensation through him. "I'm so sorry. How did you find out?"

"She stopped calling a week after I'd left for California. I sent her a bunch of text messages and called a few times a week, leaving messages and hoping I'd hear her voice again." He ground his teeth together, angry at the memory of that time.

Juliette walked closer, as if sensing he needed something to keep him upright. "Was she from your town? Maybe your parents could have let you know."

Shaking his head, Tristan said, "No, she was from another part of Paris, near the Eiffel Tower, and my parents weren't too fond of her. That was just another reason my dad wanted me to go to school outside of France, to get a good education in business and to get me away from her."

"She married your best friend. I'm sure that was tough. Did you have someone who helped you through it?"

"I didn't find out until I came home for Christmas break. I'd joined a fraternity in the fall before, and a few of my frat brothers helped me get through it when I went back for spring semester. Jackson, Roman, and Evan. Without them, I might have found a way to come home and hide for the next ten years." Tristan laughed, knowing how close to the truth it was.

He'd only been given a small allowance throughout college. His father said it would build character and help him learn how to manage his money. That allowance wouldn't cover the cost of a flight from California to France unless he saved it all for almost three months. By then, the guys had convinced him to stay, and Mr. Montgomery had helped him find a passion for marketing, something he never would have learned from his father. His mentor had seen his ability and had pushed him to develop it, creating small games for him to study people anywhere he was.

"At least you had friends stick around. Mine ditched me at one point or another."

Tristan turned to her and was surprised to see no bitterness on her face. "Is that why you know all about your parents' business? I know you spent a lot of time in the studio, but it seems like you spent a lot of time with your dad."

She nodded, giving him a close-lipped smile. "Yeah, I spent most weekends in the studio, figuring I could create something beautiful to share with the world while avoiding the gaze of so many."

"I can't believe people were so mean about something that happens to so many in the world. I didn't always have the clearest skin."

Shrugging, she said, "I'm getting to the point where I can accept it. And people change. I guess that's what I need to focus on the most. None of us are perfect, and we don't always know what's going on in other people's lives."

He thought about it and realized that even though their situations were different, he hadn't tried to change after finding out about Camila's betrayal. He'd only let the anger and fear fester within him, making it difficult to find anyone he could connect with because he wouldn't let them in.

"That's something I need to remember," he said, smiling at her. He wondered what it would be like to be free of his past. Some other problem would probably crop up, making his life just as it was now.

CHAPTER 20

*J*uliette could feel the tension knots pressing in on her shoulders. It was normal for her to get them after sitting at the pottery wheel for hours every day. It was Thursday, and she'd pushed through the past four days of throwing everything she needed to have done so it could dry in time to fire. Even creating the jewelry made her feel like the hunching of her back would turn permanent if she wasn't careful about it.

She looked around the room, missing Tristan's presence even though he'd only been gone less than an hour. With a website and several social media channels set up for the family business, he had been trying to patiently walk them through what they'd need to do for everything.

If she missed him now, what would she do when he flew to Australia? Or worse, when she had to see him all the time but not be his girlfriend?

They'd ventured out several times throughout the week, mostly at nightfall, and she found she was comfortable telling him more than she did to even Rachelle or Isabelle. Each time they were together, she felt like something connected her to him, like another small bit of rope adding itself to a bigger bond between them.

As much as she'd wanted to kiss him, she was grateful her family hadn't demanded to see them kiss. Her mother was giggly enough when she saw Tristan and Juliette holding hands. Even though Juliette knew keeping their distance was for the best, each look and half-smile he shot her made it harder to resist him. Keeping the reality of the situation at the front of her mind, she knew she had to do it.

Tristan had been through heartbreak. So had she, but in a different way. Either way, she half wished she could go back to life before this whole mess and save herself from the pain that was bound to come at the end of this.

As if reading her mind, Tristan walked into the studio, setting his laptop across the table from her. "Penny for your thoughts." He smiled at her, rubbing at the longer stubble on his face.

She smiled before looking back at the ring she was using to secure the gem on a long necklace. "Nothing that exciting. I was just thinking about what I have left to finish before next week."

She held up the completed necklace, and Tristan nodded his approval. She stood to set it with the rest of the jewelry on another shelf where she would have to package it up later. "Did you get every-thing figured out for your flight?"

"Yeah, my pilot will meet me in Rennes. I need to leave to be there by noon to make it to Sydney by Sunday night. It's going to be crazy to pack so much into four days, but I'm not missing this festival." He chuckled, and Juliette joined him, liking the deep sound of his laugh.

"Do you have to travel like this often?" she asked, placing a few of her tools back into a box. Pulling out the next gem, she looked at it for several moments, trying to decide what to create with it.

He shook his head. "No, not this far. Jackson is one of my frat brothers, as I mentioned before. He has done a lot for me, and I want to make sure his business continues to thrive. Most of the long-distance accounts are for guys from the IBC."

This was his life, traipsing around the world and seeing all the sights. He was probably ready for a busy place like Sydney after the quiet pace of Dinan.

"I'll ask my mom for the van. At least you'll sit up front this time."

She grinned at him, and he laughed before both of them quieted for a moment. She could still picture him with the wind blowing around his head as he tried to have a conversation with them on the way home from the train. At least everything in Dinan was relatively close, so they'd either walked or taken bikes to see parts of the town over the last week and a half. The only time he'd been in the van was that first day.

When Juliette glanced at him, Tristan seemed conflicted, and she wondered what would cause that. He typed on his computer for a few minutes, his brow knitted together as he concentrated on the screen. "You could come with me if you want."

Raising an eyebrow, Juliette stared at him. "To Australia?"

"Yeah, it would be nice to have you around for the long flight."

"Oh, so you just want company on the flight. What would I do for the rest of the time you were there? Twiddle my thumbs at the hotel?" She grinned at him, hoping he knew she was kidding.

Tristan didn't answer for several seconds. "No, there's a lot to do in Sydney, and Jackson's girlfriend lives there now. She's a lot of fun."

Juliette thought about it for several seconds before shaking her head. "Had it been any other time, I would have said yes. But with the timeline here, I only have a bit of time to get things done." She saw the change in his face, as if slightly disappointed. "But what if we go on an excursion tomorrow? I can work through the weekend to make up for it while you're gone."

"Are you sure?"

"Yeah, we could go up to Saint Malo and hang out there for the day. It's not far from here, and it would help me get rid of some of the knots in my shoulders." She bent over the wire, twisting it with her pliers to begin the setting.

"That would be fun. I could use some time away from the computer before cramming everything in next week." He stood and stretched. "Do you want to go for a walk?"

Tristan's question caused her head to jerk up, and she looked at him. They'd visited different haunts from Juliette's past, and each time they went out, she tried not to think of it as a date, even though in every way, they looked as though that's what they were doing.

With her emotions high, she knew she should have said no, but she found herself nodding. Checking her watch, she found it almost seven at night, much later than she'd assumed.

"Yeah. Let's pick up some food on the way back."

"That might give your mom some relief. She's been trying to figure out how to use Facebook all day, and I think she might have forgotten to watch the time to start making anything."

Juliette smiled and shook her head. "She could probably use a day off to recuperate, then. I'm sure she's overwhelmed by it all."

"Maybe they'll be able to hire one of the younger kids here to take care of all the technology after the festival. It would be extra money for the kid and peace of mind for your parents."

"That's a good idea, actually. I don't know if she'll be able to figure it all out by the time we leave here." She stood, putting away her tools before she moved next to the door. "Let me go change really quick, and I'll be right out."

She ran out the back door, untying the apron she'd forgotten to take off before leaving the studio. Her mother was standing before the fridge, a frown on her face.

Juliette stopped long enough to say, "Hey, Maman. Tristan and I are going to go out for a bit, so don't worry about dinner for us."

With a sigh of relief, her mother said, "Oh, bless you. I didn't have the energy to cook a full meal tonight."

"Well, thank you for all of the other nights when you did. Make sure to take a break and relax. We can bring something back for you if you want."

"No," her mother said, shaking her head. "I have some turkey soup in the pantry I can warm up for your father and grandfather. Go have fun." She kissed her daughter's cheeks, and Juliette turned, racing up the stairs.

CHAPTER 21

$\mathcal{L}$ooking over her piles of clothes, Juliette wasn't sure what to wear. She'd brought a variety from Paris, but this was her last night with Tristan for a few days, and she secretly wanted him to think about her while he was gone.

Throwing on a pale-blue fitted t-shirt and some clean shorts, she took a look in the mirror. She pulled her hair out of a ponytail and shook it, running her fingers through it to remove the tangles near the bottom. After adding a fresh layer of mascara, she coated her lips with a thin layer of lip balm and moved out of the room.

Her heart beat louder with each step down the stairs, and she had to focus on breathing as she walked out and saw Tristan standing with his hands in his pockets and staring up at the sky above. The sun hadn't quite set, and the sky was still lit with different colors.

"Did you have somewhere in mind?" she asked, pulling him from his thoughts.

He turned to her, a smile spreading across his face. "You look amazing." It took two—maybe three—seconds for him to close the distance and bring his lips to hers. The sensation spread through her body, like a spark spread by a wind. For someone who hadn't been in a relationship for quite a while, he sure knew how to kiss.

Pulling back slowly, she asked, "What was that for?" She reached her hand up to her forehead, trying to calm the sudden dizziness she felt.

Tristan blinked his eyes a few times as if trying to clear something from them. "The kiss. Uh, well…" He looked up at the house. "Your mother was looking through the window, so I thought it would be good." His eyes grew wide, and a smile spread across his face after the words, making him look more adorable than ever.

If only he hadn't said it was fake. She'd felt the sparks, the tingles, and whatever else people called them, but he must be a really good actor.

She gave him a close-lipped smile and turned toward the town. "I feel like pizza and then a walk after. Does that work?"

"That sounds good to me. Is there a place in town that you'd recommend?"

Changing directions slightly, they walked down a few streets, and Juliette was surprised when Tristan took her hand in his, intertwining his fingers with hers. It felt so intimate, and her brain started to spin, knowing she should disentangle herself from him and move on. But something about the peace in his expression made it so she couldn't focus on anything else.

Trying to tell herself it was all for show for the townspeople nodding and waving at them on the way, she decided she'd indulge herself for the night. He was set to leave in less than two days anyway and would probably not think about her while he was gone.

Stopping in front of a small shop, she pointed toward it. "This is it."

He stepped forward and held the door open for her. "After you."

The smell of baked bread and cheese filled her nose, causing her stomach to groan. Laughing, she said, "I think I forgot about lunch today."

"Me too," Tristan said, pulling out her chair.

She sat and helped scoot it in before he sat on the other side.

"With all of your mother's questions, I don't remember worrying about it."

After the waiter took their order, Tristan narrowed his eyes, the corners of his mouth twitching. "Other than the party fiasco, did you date anyone or have a boyfriend?"

"I've been on several dates, but none of them really went anywhere."

"Sounds about like my dating life. At least people don't analyze every move you make when you're out and about."

Juliette pulled the fabric napkin from the table and pulled out the flatware, twisting the cloth around a finger. "Yeah, you're right. I think that would make things hard all-around. How do you deal with it?"

With a sly grin, he said, "I don't read the papers."

"Huh? How can you be in marketing if you don't read what's going on in the world?"

Putting up a hand, Tristan said, "Sorry, I meant that I don't read anything that has to do with the society pages. It's been a lot easier since then, and I don't have to freeze up as my brain reminds me of all the things I've done wrong in past articles."

Juliette reached forward, resting her hand on top of his. "I'm so sorry, Tristan. That sounds rough."

"But you're an up-and-coming name. Don't you have plenty of articles written about you?"

She chuckled as she pulled her hand back. "No, not too many, thank goodness."

"I know you said you don't like the attention. What if you liked someone who was constantly scrutinized by the public? Do you think you could handle the pressure?" His stare bored into her, and she saw the earnestness of his words.

"If I knew it was for someone I loved, I would persevere through it. At least, that's my hope."

The pizza came, and the rest of their conversation moved away from such intense topics, but Juliette kept coming back to his questions. Was he asking because he was just curious and it was something to fill their time together? Or had he really wanted to know because he was starting to feel something for her?

Juliette pushed the thoughts away, hoping to enjoy this time together, knowing that dissecting every little word or nuance would drive her mad while he was away.

CHAPTER 22

$\mathcal{T}$ristan rose early the next morning, unable to sleep too long as he wondered what their outing would be like. The evening had been relaxed, which he'd needed after a day of trying to break down social media for her parents.

He could still feel the warmth of Juliette's lips on his, sparks of electricity shooting throughout. As he thought about her face after, the glassy eyes and stunned expression, he chuckled. He was grateful he'd been able to come up with the white lie that her mother was watching. Who knows? Maybe she had been, but as he looked at her in that moment, all he wanted to do was kiss her, hoping to convey that his feelings were growing stronger for her.

It had taken everything he could to keep from letting out a happy cry when she said she'd consider dating someone who was constantly in the spotlight, because he was close to all-in at that point. He just wasn't sure she felt the same.

Downstairs, he was surprised to find Juliette sitting at the table, sipping tea. A croissant sat on the table in front of her as she read something on her phone.

"You're up early," he whispered, trying not to wake up the rest of the house as the clock said 7:00 a.m.

She jumped and spun toward him. "Oh, good morning. I didn't hear you come down." He could see tiredness in her eyes and wondered if she'd slept as little as he had.

"What time are we leaving for Saint Malo?" he asked, pulling several slices of bread from the basket where it was kept and spreading jam on each. He poured himself a glass of juice and moved everything to the table, across from Juliette.

"We can head out as soon as we're done eating if you want. It's about thirty kilometers away, and we could see a lot before most of the tourists have made it out of bed."

Tristan nodded, taking a bite of his bread.

The drive to Saint Malo felt short as he and Juliette chatted about the scenery and the options for how to spend their day.

The coast was breathtaking, and Tristan realized it had been some time since he'd been to a beach. He really had been working more than he'd realized, and life was slipping by faster and faster all the time. These little moments needed to become a part of his life. He needed to give his mind a break and create memories he'd look back on years later, rather than only remembering the years by the campaigns he'd arranged.

They toured several of the sites, and Juliette looked ready to burst as she said, "Are you ready for the main surprise?"

Tristan gave her a half-smile while looking at her out of the corner of his eye. "Sure."

Her hand looped through his arm, and she pulled him toward the ocean, turning him a bit to see a structure on a small island.

"What's that?"

"Petit Bé. It's not knight-era old, but over three hundred years and still standing is pretty impressive, don't you think?" Her smile lit up her face, the rays of the sun making her eyes look as if they were sparkling.

Waving his hand out in front of them, he said, "Let's go. It sounds interesting."

She kept her hand through his arm as they walked, and something inside him felt more at peace than he had most of his adult life.

"Since it's low tide, we can walk out to the fort. It was built in the 1690s to keep the British and Dutch naval fleets from destroying Saint Malo."

Shaking his head at her, he asked, "How do you remember all this stuff?"

With a light giggle, she said, "My father is the history buff and would talk about it for hours while we worked. I used to feel nerdy, but I'm owning it now."

They walked inside, and Tristan was surprised at how amazing the place was, his favorite part being the period cannon set up at the back. One of the guides described how the fort had fallen into disrepair in the early 1900s, all the way until the year 2000 when a non-profit restored it to what it was now.

Walking back to the mainland a bit later, they trudged through the sand, and Tristan stopped for a moment, turning to look at her. "You planned this whole trip for me?"

She shrugged and nodded. "I saw how excited you were about the older stuff and thought it might be fun. Did you enjoy the fort?"

He gave her a wide grin. "Definitely. It was awesome. I just can't believe you'd do that for me."

"Why not? You haven't been to Brittany, and I wanted you to see some of the beauty around here before you had to travel for hours."

His eyes locked with hers, and he felt a zip of energy pass through his chest. Before he realized what he was doing, he cupped her head in his hands and pressed his lips to hers. A shock of sensations moved through his lips, and he pulled back to look into her eyes for a few seconds before leaning in for another kiss. It was like a drug for him, pulling him in. Not knowing exactly how she felt about everything, he relaxed a bit, leaving a few light kisses along the edge of her lips before pulling back.

Juliette looked at him with starry eyes and a shy smile. "What was that for?"

"Because you're beautiful and to say thank you."

"For what?"

He gave her a half-smile. "For being you."

Saturday morning came fast, and Tristan was packed and ready to fly out for Sydney. Juliette didn't want him to go and wondered how she would survive the people who'd been so kind with him around. It wasn't like they would be horrible to her, but the fact that Tristan was so darn attractive helped them forget about her past. With him gone, would they treat her like the recluse who'd lived in her parents' home for years?

She kept reliving the kisses from the day before, her lips feeling the same electricity she'd felt as he held her head in his hands and kissed her. It wasn't like she'd had that many kisses in her life, but this trumped all of them. And now he was leaving her. Would she make it through the next week?

Borrowing her parents' van, she drove Tristan to the Rennes airport thirty-five minutes away. "Thank you for all you've done the past two weeks. I hope you're not too far behind in work."

Tristan shook his head. "I think we'll be fine. Delegation is working a lot better than I'd expected. What about for you?"

Juliette nodded. "Seamlessly. It makes me wonder if I've just hired and trained the right people or if my job really isn't that hard."

"From what I've seen from you, you seem to be very meticulous when it comes to your work. Hasn't it been hard to be away for this long?"

Tristan's words got her thinking, and she realized he'd been watching her more than she'd expected.

Shaking her head, she said, "No, actually, which surprises me. But I think if I didn't have Rachelle, I'd be panicking and calling every hour to make sure things were done according to schedule. She's been with me since I moved to Paris, and since I first trained her, she's known almost exactly what I would want in certain situations."

"I could use someone like that. Angela is my assistant, and she does a great job with a lot of things, but the creative part isn't something she'd be interested in. Luckily, I've hired enough people who like doing that."

Pulling up to the airport, Juliette wasn't sure what to do. Her family wasn't around, but if he'd been her real boyfriend, she would get out and kiss him goodbye. Could she do that without making herself pine over him for days or months when he no longer filled this role?

She put the van in park and decided to get out to see him off. She shut the back door after he'd pulled his bag out. The bag was on the ground as he shifted his other bags into place, so she picked up the handle, trying to calm her insides a bit.

After several seconds of her heart thundering in her ears, she lifted up on tiptoe and kissed him. It wasn't long, but she realized after she pulled away that it was full of longing as she knew she would miss him over the next week.

"What was that for?" Tristan asked, a half-smile on his face.

With a shrug, she said, "I think I'll miss you while you're gone. We've done so much together that it will be weird to not have you sitting at the table in the studio."

He placed his hands just below her shoulders and pulled her closer, his lips meeting hers with an intensity she hadn't felt from him before. It wasn't a goodbye kiss, but a see-you-soon kind, making her body go light at the thought.

He pulled away and looked at her as if trying to come up with the words he wanted to say.

After a quick hug, he picked up his suitcase and wheeled it behind him into the airport, turning to wave at her before disappearing inside. She wasn't sure what had just happened exactly, but she knew she wasn't going to be the same. The slippery slope of love was claiming her, and she wasn't too worried to go down it for once in her life.

* * *

RETURNING TO HER PARENTS' home, Juliette walked out to the studio as soon as she pulled in, knowing she'd need something to distract her from the thoughts of the handsome billionaire traveling to a different continent.

She'd been leaned over for a few hours, shaping wires that would hold the gems for the jewelry she was making, her back aching from the lack of movement, when a knock came at the door.

"Come in!"

Her mother opened the door and walked over to her. "Hello, my girl. I can't believe how much you've gotten done since you arrived. How are you doing since Tristan left?"

Trying to keep back the small flood of tears, she swallowed and said, "I'm sure I'll be fine. He has to travel often, so this is one of those times where I just have to be a big girl and make it through the week." Was she supposed to feel like that? He'd been with her from morning until night for days in a row, and she didn't get sick of him. That had to be saying something.

"I know it will be hard, but the two of you are adorable together." She handed Juliette a newspaper clipping. It was a picture of her and Tristan walking along the river bank, the two of them laughing.

Juliette skimmed the text below saying something about the playboy settling down. As much as she wished she could be a permanent fixture in his life, she knew it would only last for another week or so. She could feel the pain of it already. And then to have him working on her campaigns? She just hoped he'd find someone else to head it up so she wouldn't be reminded of him all the time.

"Thanks, Maman. How is Papa?" Glancing up at her mother, she was surprised at how tired she looked. "Are you all right?"

Her mother wiped her hand over her face. "Oh, I'll be fine, my dear. Just taking things one day at a time."

Juliette leaned over and hugged her. Seeing the vulnerability there, that her parents weren't getting any younger, sent a shot of fright through her. She'd always thought they'd be there, her one constant in a world full of chaos. But from all the health struggles and life challenges thrown at them, she realized the future was a mystery.

Pulling back, Juliette said, "If I haven't said it enough, thank you. You and Papa have always taken such good care of us, and I haven't always been the most grateful child."

Her mother reached out and touched her face, tucking a stray hair behind her ear. "Aw, my dear. Life has dealt you quite a lot, but you're stronger for it, much stronger than you can imagine."

Juliette teared up. It was the first real compliment she'd ever had from her mother that didn't have some backhanded slight to it. Not that she usually meant to come across like that. She just expected a lot of herself and required the same of her family.

"I have dinner on the stove. I'd better go check on it. Make sure to take time out to eat." She wagged her finger in front of Juliette's face, causing Juliette to laugh.

"I'm beat. I think I'll come in now and wash up."

She followed her mother out of the shop and into the house where she jogged up the stairs to her room. As she sat on her bed, she noticed the spotted shirt Tristan had borrowed from her father. Was it possible she could miss someone so terribly after only knowing them a couple of weeks?

She took a quick shower and tied her long hair into a ponytail. Picking up her phone from the bed, she was surprised to find a text from Tristan that he'd sent only an hour after leaving.

Made it to Paris. We're refueling to make it the long leg to Hong Kong. Hope you're doing well. It feels weird not having you here right now.

Juliette's pulse ramped up, and she turned, falling onto the bed. She looked at the ceiling, wondering what to write back.

I've been working in the shop, or I would've called. I hope you weren't too bored. Call me when you get to Australia.

She reread her text at least a dozen times, debating whether or not to keep the last line in it. Pushing send, she smiled, a shot of excitement exploding in her chest as she thought of all the possibilities. She knew she shouldn't have feelings for him, but she couldn't help but fantasize what it would be like to be his real girlfriend, or even his wife one day.

It had been days since she'd been on the Quickstagram app for Rousseau Belle, so she clicked on it, scrolling through likes and comments, making sure to respond to each. On an older picture of her, she found a comment from Tristan, and she knew she was in danger.

I miss this face.

Looking at the timestamp, it was around the same time as he'd sent the text.

"Juliette! Dinner's ready," her mother called up the stairs.

Juliette sighed, already wishing Tristan was on his way back from Australia.

Walking down the stairs, she wondered if she should expect the same kind of contact a normal boyfriend and girlfriend would have while apart. She hoped that would happen, but there was only so much her heart could take. Going slowly would be the best course of action.

CHAPTER 24

By the time his flight was about to land in Sydney on Sunday, Tristan felt as though he'd been hit by a truck. He'd slept here and there, but nothing to help him feel refreshed. Looking at his watch, he was grateful it was later at night so he had an excuse to head to the hotel and collapse.

He'd spent a lot of travel time working on answering emails and refining the changes he'd be implementing once he touched down in Sydney. It was going to be a tight visit, trying to get everything in that he needed to. Feeling accomplished after the first long leg of the journey, his phone had died halfway through the flight, even after using his remote charger. He wished he'd brought a book from the Rousseau's collection to keep him occupied.

After landing in Sydney, Tristan plugged in his phone and found a text from Jackson.

I have a car on its way. Hailey's boss arrived a bit earlier, so you'll have to share with him. Sorry, mate.

He glanced at the time on his phone. 9:03 p.m. After twenty-plus hours of traveling, he wasn't in the mood to chat, and Americans were always chatty. Like his friend, Evan Pearson, who never shut up. At least he liked the guy.

The black car arrived, and Tristan slipped inside, nodding to the guy next to him. Grateful for Jackson's warning, he was able to prepare himself. As the guy spoke, Tristan realized he wasn't as put off by the openness as he would've been had he stayed in Paris. The people of Dinan seemed to be more open and welcoming than most of the Parisians he knew, and that small tidbit made him curious.

"What are you in Australia for?" the man asked, smiling at him. He was dressed in a suit, and Tristan shifted, knowing he had to be uncomfortable. Even though he wore one every day for work, when he traveled, he preferred slacks and a polo, sometimes even dressing down in jeans. A full three-piece suit added enough warmth without recirculated air in a confined space. And when arriving this late at night, comfort made him less cranky.

"Work," Tristan said, pulling out one of his earbuds he'd left in from the flight. He wasn't used to conversing for long periods of time with strangers unless it had to do with marketing.

The man smiled. "Me too. I'm Jonathan. My real estate company set up a branch here in Sydney, so I'm heading to check it out."

Tristan nodded, giving him a small smile, trying to figure out why that information would be familiar to him. "Oh, that's right. Jackson said you were Hailey's boss."

"How do you know Jackson?" The man narrowed his eyes as if studying Tristan.

"We go way back to college. Delta Phi."

Jonathan grinned. "He's a great guy. I only met him at the beginning of the year when he was looking for property in California. Since we set up this branch in May, I haven't been out yet to check on how things are going, but from how it sounds, Hailey is killing it."

Tristan shrugged. "I only get my news about her second-hand, and Jackson isn't always a reliable storyteller. But with everything I know about Hailey, I believe it to be true. She's a good one."

"That she is. What do you have planned once we check in at the hotel?" Jonathan asked.

Shaking his head, Tristan said, "Probably just head to my room and crash. It's been a long trip. Probably a lot longer for you. How long was your journey?"

Jonathan smiled. "I'm working with someone in Germany to expand our brand there too, so it was shorter than it would've been from California. I'll basically have traveled around the world in about two weeks."

With a guy this ambitious, Tristan couldn't help but pull a card out of his wallet. "I'm Tristan Delacroix, and I own Delacroix—"

"Marketing. No way! It's so good to meet you. I've heard a lot of good things about your company. I guess you do international campaigns, then, since you're flying to Australia."

"We've done a few. I'm working to expand into the beauty industry at the moment and know that will be an adventure in and of itself. But if you're looking for a good marketing company, even if it's just for the foreign sites, let us give you a bid and some examples of what we can do for your brand."

"Will do."

The car stopped, and Tristan looked out the window, feeling the exhaustion set in as he saw the hotel. He could use a shower and a good night's sleep. Even with the time difference, it wouldn't be hard to fall asleep once he got to his room.

As the two of them got out of the car and came around to the trunk for their luggage, Jonathan turned to him. "Do you know of any bars or clubs here in Sydney?"

Tristan hadn't been to any when he'd come to Australia, usually only having time to work and hang out with Jackson as much as possible. On a Sunday night, he wasn't sure what would be open.

Shaking his head, he said, "I'm sorry. I'm sure there are people here who would know." He readjusted the strap of his laptop case, wishing the driver would hurry so he could get to his room.

"You should come out with me. It's no fun to go to new places by yourself."

Shifting again, Tristan glanced at him a moment before saying, "I don't drink, so that might put a damper on things."

"Don't drink?" The look on Jonathan's face made Tristan wish they hadn't even started speaking.

"I quit in college."

Jonathan seemed to study Tristan's profile. "Well, just join me for a soda, then. I don't want to be alone on my first night here."

What did he have to lose? Maybe they could be out for an hour and he could still try to recuperate from the long flight. He needed to get a lot done in the short time frame before the festival, and he was surprised at how much he'd rather be there right now than in Sydney.

"Fine. But I've got a long day tomorrow. I won't be staying long."

"Awesome. Thanks, man." Jonathan grinned, and Tristan wished he could wipe it off him. Something about the guy didn't sit well but Tristan couldn't place it.

With a guarded smile, Tristan nodded, hoping he'd be able to get this over with as soon as possible.

CHAPTER 25

After checking into the hotel, Tristan had mixed feelings that Jonathan was staying only a few floors below him. There was something about this guy that made him a little wary. It had been so long since he'd had a drink that every time he walked into a bar, the smell caught him off guard and he had to breathe through his mouth.

The hotel concierge had recommended this place only a block away from the hotel, and Tristan had opted for it. Close meant not having to drive and being able to leave whenever he wanted to.

Jonathan ordered a whiskey while Tristan asked for a club soda. Pulling out his phone, he wanted to talk to Juliette, but he hadn't had time to charge the battery. The black screen taunted him, and he slipped it back into his pants pocket.

"What's the story behind the sobriety?" Jonathan asked, sipping from the glass in front of him. His voice was louder than normal since the music was blaring from the overhead speakers. Tristan could feel a pounding headache taking form.

Looking at the guy, Tristan wasn't sure he wanted to share the story. After a minute of indecision, he said, "I was in a fraternity in college, like I told you before, and we drank all night and ended up trashing the hotel rooms. Our house mentor talked the hotel out of

124

pressing charges on the terms that we wouldn't drink again and that we replace everything that was broken. Shortly after that, one of the guys died after driving drunk. He took the lives of a small family as well. I've just never missed the stuff since then."

Shrugging his shoulders, Jonathan said, "That was a long time ago. Don't you think you've done your penance?"

Tristan nodded. "Yes, it's been more than paid, but it was something we all agreed to. I just don't have a desire to break that anymore." He didn't need to tell the guy that giving up drinking was one of the best things he'd done in his life. He never had to worry about a fuzzy memory or inappropriate behavior, both of which happened too often to remember during his first year of college, especially after Camila. It was a way to honor Mr. Montgomery as well, especially now that he'd passed on.

Tristan hadn't been without awkward moments in his time since, as most of his family and friends had a glass of wine with most of their meals. He didn't judge them for it, only knowing he was probably better off without it.

Some girls walked up to the bar, ordering some drinks, and Tristan turned toward the wall of bottles in front of him, hoping to avoid their gaze.

Jonathan struck up a conversation with them, and as much as Tristan wanted to leave, something kept him rooted to the chair. Maybe it was the fact that Jonathan seemed like a naïve tourist and Tristan should be the designated walker since they'd come there on foot.

He'd effectively tuned out the conversation for long enough that Jonathan had to hit him on the shoulder to get his attention, pulling his thoughts from the girl with the deep sea-blue eyes.

"These two want to dance. You coming?" Jonathan said, his smile crooked. Buzzed but not drunk, yet.

"I think I'll just stay here. It's been a long day of traveling."

One girl smiled even wider. "Oh, you're French. That's so attractive." She walked up and put her hands on his face, pulling him in and kissing him on the lips. He was surprised by her grip because it took some force to pull away from her.

"I'm dating someone right now. Thanks, but no, I won't dance tonight." Throwing back the rest of his drink, he paid his tab and walked out the door. He loved nothing more than the thought of taking ibuprofen and sleeping until morning to cure the thundering in his mind.

CHAPTER 26

Juliette tried not to focus on the fact that Tristan hadn't called in over two days. She knew that most of the first twenty-four hours were probably spent flying, and with the time change, she tried to give him the benefit of the doubt. But thoughts started to creep in, making her wonder if she'd just imagined everything they'd had the past two weeks. She pulled up his comment on her post, reminding herself of the factual evidence for what she'd been feeling.

She'd gotten up early that Monday morning, hoping to finish out the work she needed to do before the festival began on Saturday.

After pacing back and forth several times in the shop, she clicked on his name, telling herself she was only being a good fake girlfriend. She just needed to know he'd made it safely there. If she went to lunch with no information on his whereabouts, her mother would get suspicious and start fishing for answers.

The dial tone sounded, seeming louder than normal. After five rings, she was sure it would go to voicemail, when his voice came on the line, a bit rushed. "Hello?"

"Tristan?"

"Juliette." She could hear the smile in his tone. "It's so good to hear your voice."

"You too. I just wanted to make sure you made it to Sydney in one piece. I was beginning to worry when you didn't call." Biting her lip, she waited, hoping he wouldn't think she was too forward.

Papers shuffled in the background, and he said, "Yes, sorry. My phone died on the plane, and I got this huge headache and forgot to charge it once I got to the hotel. I've been going like crazy since I got here, and I'm still at Jackson's office. It's nine here, so it's lunchtime at home. I'm hoping to get everything wrapped up before I fly back." He paused for a moment, and Juliette didn't know what to say, when he spoke again. "How are things there?"

"Good. Things are good. I'm feeling confident about the amount of dishware we've finished. The jewelry still has a long way to go, but I have several days to get it finished."

"That's great. How is Rousseau Belle? Still alive and well?"

Something about his comment rubbed her the wrong way, and she said, "Yep," her tone clipped. Did he only care about her company and that stupid contract? Was that the reason for all the little extra bits of affection?

A woman's voice echoed through the phone line, and the irritation spread through her upper body. Why was she so suspicious of his actions all of a sudden? It wasn't like he was hers after all. Maybe he really was a playboy and had only been playing the part the past couple of weeks.

"Hey, Juliette, Hailey is here. I've got to go. I'll talk to you tomorrow?" She heard the question in his words and wondered if he was sincere.

Unsure what to say, she said, "Sure. Talk to you then."

Hanging up the phone, she put it on the table, deciding to see if he would actually call her. With her emotions frayed, she headed outside, determined to go for a walk to burn off some of the steam. This was not how she'd expected to feel about the billionaire, but the further she kept her thoughts and feelings from him, the better off she'd be.

CHAPTER 27

Tristan had gotten up Thursday morning and felt like he'd been running since the morning after he'd landed in Sydney. With so much to get approved by Jackson and then implementing the ideas, he was glad he'd been the one to handle it, knowing it got done and done well for his friend's company.

His thoughts often strayed to Juliette, wondering what she would be doing throughout the day. He'd only had time to send a few texts here and there, the time to return her call never happened until mornings, which meant it was really late in France. He just hoped everything was running smoothly with the products for the festival and that she wouldn't hate him for not getting the chance to call.

He'd loved the fact that she'd called him just to check up. Did that mean she had feelings for him? Or was it another part of the charade for her parents? He hoped she felt something for him, because all he could think about was the kiss the night they walked together and again when they'd gone to Saint Malo.

Out to lunch at a burger place with Jackson and Hailey, Tristan was torn between wanting to vomit at the closeness and PDA they shared and wishing he had someone like Hailey. Thoughts of Juliette surfaced, and he smiled, picturing her as carefree as she had been throughout his time in Dinan.

"What's the grin for, Tristan? And if you say it's about some marketing scheme you've been working on, I'm going to call your bluff." Jackson pointed at him with his finger, a smirk covering his face.

"Just some thoughts."

"How are things in Dinan? Or is that where your mind is right now?" Jackson smirked.

Hailey turned to look at Jackson, a confused expression on her face. "What haven't you told me?"

Jackson's smirk turned into an all-out grin, and Tristan swirled the straw in his drink. "Tristan has a fake girlfriend."

Her mouth dropped open, and her eyes grew almost as wide as the plates before them. "Okay, so do you have feelings for her?"

Frowning, Tristan wasn't sure he was ready for another American to poke around in his love life. Even though he thought the world of Hailey, the discomfort he still felt about the night out with Jonathan made him bristle. At least he hadn't seen the man since that night. Hailey had spent plenty of time talking about their meetings, so Tristan knew he'd made it out of the bar alive.

"She's a nice girl. I'm playing her boyfriend until after a medieval festival her town is having this weekend."

"What do you get out of the deal?" she asked, dipping a fry into some weird condiment concoction she called "fry sauce."

"The contract to do the marketing for her company." He'd thought about it several times, always excited about the prospect to grow his company, but for some reason, he felt something like stomach acid burning his throat. Something about it wasn't so appealing now that his feelings for Juliette seemed to be growing by the day. Even though he'd been far away, he still thought of her more often than he cared to admit.

Hailey moved her finger in circles in front of his face. "I'm sensing some hesitation from you. You like her, don't you?"

Tristan scrunched up his face, closing his eyes so he wouldn't have to look at the happy expressions on both of their faces.

"What's wrong, man? I thought you'd be happy to have found someone you like who isn't all about the billions in your bank account."

He opened his eyes at Jackson's serious tone to see that his face had turned somber. Tristan was grateful to not have to worry about the continued joking.

"I like her, a lot. But now I'm worried she might not feel the same. What if it's just an act for her parents and she doesn't want a relationship?"

The two of them laughed, and Hailey brushed her hands off and said, "Tristan, the best person to ask is the girl. Sometimes a little honesty saves you a lonely trip around the sun. You of all people should know that from our experience." She moved her finger back and forth between her and Jackson.

That was true. They'd almost broken up at a gala last January because Jackson's ex-girlfriend had shown up. Tristan was glad Jackson had been able to smooth things over, because he hadn't wanted to pick his friend up after another heartbreak.

Tristan was grateful for her words, knowing in his gut it was true. But was that something he should do over the phone? Maybe better to wait until they were face to face again so he wouldn't have to worry about slow connections and miscommunication through texts.

He smiled when Jackson changed the subject, even if it was to surfing.

"Tomorrow's the day, T. We're getting you in the water and up on that board if we have to be out there all day."

Groaning, Tristan wondered if there was something else he could do instead. Fake sick? Jackson knew Tristan rarely got sick, and it would take more convincing than that if he wanted to get out of it. Maybe he could give surfing one more shot. If he couldn't stay on the board this time, he'd throw in the towel.

"I have to fly out by three at the latest tomorrow afternoon. I'm not missing that festival."

CHAPTER 28

With the employees mostly trained on the new procedures, the banners and posters hung throughout the store, and the website updated with the latest ad slogan, Tristan was happy he'd been able to accomplish so much in just a few days. It was Friday, and his flight was leaving for France that afternoon, which made him even happier.

Getting up earlier than dawn to head out to the cold water wasn't something he was so excited about. He clicked open his phone, hoping to see a text or missed call from Juliette. She was probably elbow-deep in clay and couldn't send anything.

Opening up a text, he tried to think of what he could say to test out the waters for the future that awaited him in once he landed back in France tomorrow morning.

Taking a picture of the line of bright light on the horizon, he sent it to her, sending the words, *Wish you were here*, after a short internal debate.

He walked out onto the sand, feeling it between his toes, and a peaceful feeling came over him. A text came through a minute later.

Me too.

The simple words settled into his chest as he sat on the sand.

Would someone like Juliette fall for him? He'd been through so many emotions since they'd met that he still couldn't believe how much of a pull she had on him. But did it go both ways?

He thought of Camila, of how he'd felt after finding out she'd married his then best friend. He'd carried that anger with him for so long, but what had he known at eighteen? Picturing himself as a freshman in college, he could almost visually see the changes, both inside and out, that he'd made in that time. Would he have chosen Camila now if she'd given him that chance? He'd never know, but maybe it was time to take a chance on love again. Whatever happened, he was older now, with more experience in dealing with heartbreak. He just hoped he didn't have to actually use the information.

After slapping Tristan on the back, Jackson sat on his heels and looked over at him. "I'm surprised you beat me here. Look at you, early bird."

Jackson's words brought back the memory of Juliette calling him a… "Worm catcher," Tristan said aloud.

Jackson turned to look at him, confused. "Huh?"

"It's just something Juliette said when I first met her." Tristan waved him off, standing up and looking out over the waves building in the distance, making their way to shore. Blowing out a breath, he turned and said, "Let's get to it. I've still got a couple of things I need to finish before I catch a plane to France."

With a grin, Jackson said, "I think I like this side of you. Even more blunt, and you're focused on what you need to do. Does that mean I get a discount on billable hours?"

Tristan punched him in the shoulder and said, "You already get a discount, idiot. Where are the boards? I may as well put myself in danger now rather than later. I've got someone I need to chat with about a relationship."

Jackson signaled to follow him to his car where two boards were strapped to the top of it. Loosening the hooks, Tristan pulled the lime-green board down and smirked. "What? Are you making me learn on your girlfriend's board?"

"No, hers is yellow. Just stop whining, and let's get out there."

Thirty minutes later, Tristan lay panting on his board, exhausted from the constant swimming against the current and then, with it, usually needing to pull himself up on his board.

He could hear the water lapping around him and knew Jackson was getting closer.

"Come on, man. Get this next wave. You'll be able to ride it all the way to shore if you catch it just right."

Sitting up, he twisted his head to look back, seeing the wave back twenty feet or so. He waited a few more seconds before paddling hard and slipping his legs up to the position Jackson had told him every time they'd tried this, even back in college. Working to keep his balance, he bent at the knees, trying to steer as best as he could with his feet.

Then the board cut back into the water too much, flipping the board and Tristan underwater. He pulled hard at the water, breaking the surface just as another wave came crashing down. A moment of panic filled him and he did his best to clear his mind, willing himself not to give into the water. Taking a second, he called up every ounce of strength he had and made it above water, the air burning his lungs as it went in.

It took several minutes for him to be able to climb onto his board and even longer to make it to shore, but he was officially spent. Jackson pushed him the last few yards and made sure to get it to where the sand wasn't slipping back into the water as much. Tristan wasn't sure how long he lay there, but it was long enough for Jackson to make a few more runs and be ready to head out.

"Don't talk me into doing that ever again," Tristan said, his voice hoarse.

"You got it, T. You can do a lot of things, but I think surfing is officially off the list." Jackson's smile looked as though he were trying to be reassuring, but Tristan only felt exhaustion.

Dragging the board to Jackson's vehicle, Tristan struggled to get it up high enough to go on the top and left it for Jackson to strap on. "Drop me off at the hotel. I'm going to need a shower before I head out."

Waving goodbye to Jackson at the entrance to the hotel, Tristan stumbled over to the elevator and made it to his room where he enjoyed the refreshing hot water of a shower. Packing up what little he'd brought, he waited for the car to take him to the airport. He just wished the journey was shorter so he could tell Juliette how much he cared for her.

CHAPTER 29

On Friday, with the family stand set up along the street, Juliette placed everything in crates, making sure they were properly padded with newspapers, not willing to take a chance that something would break on the short drive to the middle of Dinan. Even though the festival didn't start until the next morning, she was grateful they could get the bulk of everything set up so when the morning rush hit the booths, she wouldn't be scrambling to organize and work with the customers at the same time.

She'd loaded the van as full as she could, leaving the rest of the wares in the studio for day two if they were needed. After she'd seen all of the numbers Tristan had inputted into a spreadsheet from years past, she was surprised by how much her father had already completed, or at least started, before she'd arrived. His health had improved some, enough to allow him behind the booth for short spurts of time.

Juliette's thoughts kept drifting to a tall, dark-haired man with eyes like pools of chocolate, and she looked up every so often, as if he would come striding across the street. From what she remembered of his itinerary, he would probably be in the air now, arriving sometime the next morning.

Her brother Henri drove the van to the spot to help her unload all the crates. He had arrived with his family a few days before, and it had been so refreshing to play with his young kiddos. His wife, Rosalie, and the kids were helping Juliette's mother with getting all the merchandise set up around the table, most likely causing more ruckus than usual with the excitement of the festival.

"How have things been, Jules?" Henri asked. "Mom says the skin care stuff is doing well. Rose loves your products and is always raving about them to everyone."

Juliette smiled, picturing her eight-month-pregnant sister-in-law waddling around the town where they lived, telling everyone about the Rousseau Belle night cream or lip balm. If only Juliette had a few thousand of those kinds of people, everything would be word of mouth. Would her brand grow as quickly, though? Probably not.

"Things are good. Rachelle called yesterday to tell me that one of the night creams we've been trying to perfect for a couple of months has passed all the tests the researchers threw at it, so I hope it continues to go well when I get back."

"That's good. I'm proud of you and all you've accomplished."

"It probably helps that you don't have to pretend we're not related, huh?"

As Henri held up a hand, she saw the hurt in his eyes. "I did that one time, and I said I was sorry, Jules. When are you going to forgive me for it?"

"Now," she said. All of her grudges from her past were overdue to be forgiven, and as she said the word, a lightness filled her. She looked down at her phone, clicking it on and seeing no new notifications, so she clicked it off again. The last text had come through around two in the morning and woken her up. But the idea that he was thinking about her when looking at such a beautiful landscape, with the beach, the ocean, and the sunrise all right there, had given her some wonderful dreams for the rest of the night.

"Tell me about this boyfriend of yours."

The questioning tone of his voice caused her to jump, and she turned toward him as they parked. After getting out, they pulled open the van doors, and each took a couple of crates and walked to the table where their mother fussed that one of the plates wasn't sitting up as it should.

Juliette thought about Tristan…the soft manly scent of his cologne, the smile he flashed her when he was teasing, and the kisses they'd shared—the part she thought about most often.

"He's sweet, kind, and knows a lot about business and marketing, which will help my company when I let them do the ads for us."

"That sounds about as romantic as getting run over by a train."

Juliette laughed, grateful Henri had always known how to say things well on the first try. "He does his best to help out, and how can a girl turn that down?"

They were walking back to the van, when Henri stopped, pulling out his own phone. "I've been debating whether or not to show you this, but I just thought you'd want to see what was in the local paper this morning. They referenced that the picture was taken a few days ago."

Juliette stood confused, wondering what it was he wanted to show her. The headline read, "Back to being a playboy! What happened to the other girl?"

"Other girl?" She scrolled up, skimming what she could and reading fast when she needed a better understanding. It wasn't until the picture came into view that Juliette understood what was going on. A picture had been snapped of a woman kissing a man who looked an awful lot like Tristan.

She turned to her brother. "I'm assuming that's Tristan, or you wouldn't be showing it to me."

Henri looked at her with pity, much the same way people had done back when her face looked like spaghetti sauce. "It's in the paper in Paris but hasn't made it out this far. For your sake, I hope it doesn't come this way."

Tears pooled in the corners of her eyes, and she felt as if someone had ripped off a section of her heart, as if it were paper. "Thanks, Henri. I appreciate this." Chewing on the side of her mouth, she said, "We aren't really dating."

Her brother stopped in his tracks and turned to look at her, his expression curious if she was telling the truth. "He's not even your boyfriend?"

Closing her eyes, Juliette breathed in deep. "No, you know how Mom and Dad can get. I made up a boyfriend a few months ago. Everything was going well until Mom started guilt tripping me into bringing him. Tristan wanted the marketing contract for Rousseau Belle, and so he's pretending to be dating me to assuage the problem with the parents."

"But that isn't helping you, is it? You're in love with him."

Sitting on the bumper at the back of the van, she wiped away a tear with her fingers. "I think I am. I thought he was better than this," she said, waving her hand around the phone to emphasize her point.

As Henri wrapped her in his arms, Juliette was grateful for the small bonding moment, needing all the strength she could muster as she handed him back the phone.

"You'll find someone, Jules. Just don't tell my wife you want the most random qualities in a husband, because she somehow manages to find all of them. Less blind dates for you is a good thing when it comes to her." He chuckled, and Juliette laughed good and hard, helping to ease some of the pain.

"What am I supposed to do about him? He's coming here in a few hours. I just wish I could kick him out of Dinan and move on with my life."

A mischievous grin spread across her brother's face, and he finally said, "I have a better idea. It's like revenge, only you're not doing anything about it."

Juliette's chest pounded, hoping his idea wouldn't backfire like all the times it did as a kid. Henri was known for being mischievous, but he somehow managed to persuade his siblings to be the testers of his plans, making it so each of them took the brunt of the blame.

After a few more minutes of thought, she said, "Okay, as long as it doesn't cause any long-term damage, I'm in."

CHAPTER 30

Tristan's woke with a start, realizing he'd fallen asleep on the bed when putting his socks on. His phone buzzed on the nightstand, and he picked it up, seeing it was almost three in the afternoon.

"Hello?"

"Is everything okay, sir? I've been trying to call for the past hour. I was going to ask the front desk to check your room if you didn't answer just now."

Silas, Tristan's pilot, was known for being on time to everything, and with his calm demeanor, not much phased him. The slight worry in his voice made Tristan smile, even though he knew he needed to hurry out.

"You said you wanted to fly out by three this afternoon, correct?" Silas asked.

"I'm sorry, Silas. I must have fallen asleep. I'll be down in about five minutes and will head over from there."

Tristan had to throw his clothes into his suitcase and run out the door. Of course, the Sydney traffic was at peak rush, making it seem as though they were crawling at a snail's pace as the driver of the car Jackson had sent wove through the city to get to the airport.

The adrenaline that had poured through him when he'd realized he was late was starting to fade, and he did what he could to stay awake, focusing on the airport ahead. His body felt a little more rested, but there were already aching spots where he was sure he'd hit rocks or something.

Once at the small airport, Silas got to work checking everything for their flight. After refueling and all the prechecks, they were airborne within thirty minutes.

After the plane reached cruising altitude, Tristan stood and walked to the small kitchen to fill a glass with water. He guzzled it and filled it once more, sipping slower this time. His thirst must have been from surfing that morning and then not refueling. Poking around in the cabinets, he found some biscuits and pulled out a few, curbing his hunger for a bit.

Sitting back in his seat, he was again surprised by the amount of exhaustion he'd felt. Was this why his father had decided to retire? There were times when Tristan was a child that he didn't see his father for a week or more as he worked late at the office. After only getting a couple of hours of sleep every night while in Sydney, it was taking its toll on him.

Angela's words came back to him, making him realize he needed to delegate to his employees to make it so he wasn't working himself toward a heart attack.

After the festival, he'd relax, go on a vacation somewhere and not work a stitch. Maybe he could convince Juliette to come with him.

The time seemed to move slower with each hour, and after they stopped to refuel, Tristan felt like a child counting down until his birthday.

Once he stepped off the plane in Rennes early Saturday morning, he could barely contain his excitement, sending Juliette a quick text to say they'd touched down. He'd sent her a text before he left on the last leg, giving her an estimate of when the plane would land so she could meet him at the airport. He hadn't received a response, and a feeling of panic took hold until he remembered she was most likely busy with the family booth and probably didn't have her phone on her.

A car waited near the hangar where Tristan kept his jet, but it wasn't Juliette or her mom's van. The man got out of the car and took Tristan's bag, placing it into the trunk.

"May I ask who you are?" Tristan asked.

The man shifted, looking him up and down as if he were ready for a fight. "I'm Henri, Juliette's brother. She got busy with the festival preparation, so she sent me to get you."

Tristan nodded. "Thanks. It's good to finally meet you. Juliette talks a lot about you and your other brother and how she's the favorite aunt."

Henri chuckled. "She does a really good job being an aunt; that's for sure." He opened the back door, and Tristan felt odd having Juliette's brother chauffeur him.

"I'll sit up front if you don't mind."

Something like surprise flashed across Henri's eyes, and he nodded. "Sure." He moved to open the front door, but Tristan got it first, sliding in and shutting the door by himself.

The drive back to Dinan seemed to take even longer than most of the flights, and he just wanted to get there and see Juliette, to tell her how much he cared for her, even after only a few weeks.

Her brother must have sensed his anticipation, because he asked, "Are you excited about something?"

"Only to see Juliette. It's been a few days, and I missed her." Tristan saw Henri looking a bit confused.

"Well, she has a surprise for you. It could be quite the adventure, though." He gave Tristan what looked like a grimace before focusing back on the road.

They had to take a back road to get to Juliette's parents' house. When they got there, Tristan hurried and took his suitcase inside and then glanced around a bit, before realizing she must be at the festival.

"Where is the booth?" he asked Henri. "I need to talk to her as soon as possible."

The man responded with, "In the main square. It's about a kilometer from here, but it's better to walk than try to drive in this mess. We won't get anywhere with everything blocked off."

Jogging to the square, Tristan tried to prepare what questions he would ask and what he would say overall. He would reveal his feelings for her, and at least that bit of anxiety would go away.

The market was crowded with people at only nine in the morning, surprising him. He stood on tiptoe, scanning the people behind each booth and finally finding her about halfway down. With her bright smile and blue irises, Tristan knew he'd fallen for his fake girlfriend. When or how it had happened, he wasn't sure, but he was happier than ever that they'd met.

Stepping into line, his brain buzzed about how he could start the conversation. He'd still not made a decision by the time he was first in line.

She turned, her long ponytail whipping to one side of her and then the other. "What can I help—Oh, hello." Her tone was cold, icy even. He wasn't sure what had happened. She'd been more than courteous to the people before him. What had changed so rapidly? He racked his brain, trying to think of something he'd done wrong.

"Hey. I couldn't wait to see you." He looked around the booth, amazed by the stacks of crates filled with things she made.

She rubbed her lips together, pulling his attention to them, and he wanted to lunge over the table and kiss her.

"It's good to see you too. I'm glad you made it back safe." Her smile looked forced, causing Tristan to wonder what was off. "Mathieu has your costume ready, and I think you'll be up soon."

Glancing around, he tried to connect her words to the things he knew about the festival. "Up for what?"

Her smile looked almost sad then, and she just said, "You'll see," before looking at someone over his shoulder and asking what she could do for them.

Standing in the middle of the square, he couldn't figure out what had happened between him and Juliette or what she wanted him to do now. Soon enough, two guys grabbed him, one being Henri and the other looking like he fit into the family. Tristan assumed it was Mathieu, Juliette's other brother.

"Where are we going? Juliette said something about being up?"

Tristan turned to both of them, hoping they would explain the situation to him.

They made their way through town and let him go before what looked like a large arena. Both of Juliette's brothers dropped large bags they'd been carrying on their shoulders, and Tristan wasn't sure what that had to do with him being "up."

"Put this on," Henri said, throwing him a pile of clothes.

Tristan held them out, trying to figure out what they were for, and saw several men walk past dressed in period costumes. As he opened his mouth to ask where to change, both brothers pointed to a wall behind him, which turned out to be port-a-potties.

It took a little work to get it to all fit, and the bottoms of the pants were still shorter than he was used to, making him look more like a clown than anything. Stepping out of the small enclosed space, he was grateful for the fresh air and breathed in deeply, hoping to get rid of the smell that seemed to cling to him in these clothes.

"Okay, I'm dressed. What's next?"

Again, the men seemed to be mute, even though he'd had a full conversation with Henri on the way over just a half-hour before. Opening the other bag, they pulled out several pieces of armor, securing them around the designated body parts. The pieces seemed too small for his stature, and Tristan hoped it was just for show and not for competition.

Once everything had been connected and tightened, Henri handed him a helmet and asked, "Have you ever ridden a horse?"

"It's been a while, but yes. I rode a lot as a kid."

He nodded, motioning for Tristan to follow him. Walking around the wall, they came upon an area where there were several tools and long staffs. A long line of wood was set up in the middle, and at first, Tristan got excited. He would be able to see all the action from here.

Mathieu reappeared with a horse, already saddled. Tristan rubbed his hand over the horse's face, making it nuzzle further into his hand. "That's a good boy."

An announcer came over the line. "Welcome back to another

jousting match for this weekend. Our first contestants for this round are Jacques Avelline against Tristan Delacroix."

What? He was the one competing? He looked from the horse to the armor and over to where Henri now held out a long, thick pole.

The crowd cheered, the sound so loud, and Tristan wondered if all of this was worth it. Was careening down a straight line on a horse, holding out a stick longer than he was tall as he tried to hit another guy doing the same thing, going to help him figure out why Juliette was so cross with him? If anything, he'd probably end up with a concussion.

As if numb, he slowly placed his foot into the stirrup and swung a leg around. Sitting in the saddle, he looked over at Mathieu, who had a lance in his hands. "Go get him. You'll need to hold the lance steady once it hits because the impact will pull it in all directions."

Slipping the helmet on his head, Tristan shut the flap of metal over the eye slit and tightened his grip on the lance. The flags waved in the middle, and without prompting, the horse took off, causing Tristan to lose his balance for a half a second before he righted himself and focused on the man in front of him.

All he could remember about jousting was what he'd learned from the movie *A Knight's Tale*. Before he knew it, the two of them collided, and Tristan felt the impact down to his core. The horse trotted back to the beginning, and Tristan made to disembark.

"What are you doing?" Henri asked.

"I'm getting off the horse. I survived one crash. I need to speak to Juliette, but something was off about her. Do you know what's going on?" Tristan made sure to give them a serious look, because being thrown into all of this was something he hadn't expected after more than a day of traveling back.

"You can't get off the horse. You still have to joust again. You earned a point on that round, but if you give up now, the other guy wins." Henri was practically begging at this point, and Tristan wondered why he was all of a sudden so worried about it.

Thinking about it, Tristan finally said, "If I finish this round, will you tell me what's going on?"

The two brothers looked at one another, communicating with a few grunts and nods of the head.

"If you stay in this round, we'll tell you a bit about what's going on," Mathieu said. "The rest, you'll have to solve on your own."

Gripping a new lance, Tristan charged forward, this time at his signal rather than the horse's, not truly believing he was riding down a strip of ground with a lance in his hand.

His heartbeat was pounding in his face as he focused on the guy coming at him, not wanting to completely miss. His lance hit home around the stomach, picking the guy up from the horse and dropping him on the ground. The crowd went wild, and Tristan was glad he didn't have to make a living on fighting. The impact reverberated down his arms and into his body. He'd be even more sore tomorrow.

As Tristan trotted the brown-and-white horse back, he rubbed her neck and then slid off, coming face to face with the horse's face, and he had to force himself to be nice. Folding his arms as best he could with all the armor on, he looked between the two brothers. "Well? What is going on, and why am I jousting?"

"First of all, what are your feelings and intentions toward our sister?" Henri asked. He narrowed his eyes at Tristan, causing the latter to shift back a few steps.

Taking a deep breath, Tristan said, "I like her, a lot. I mean, we've only known each other for three weeks, but I really like her. I might even love her."

The older brother turned to Henri and said, "See? I told you he had feelings for her."

Turning back to Tristan, Henri said, "Did you see this?" He handed him a phone with a picture on it.

As the details slowly entered Tristan's mind, he realized it was that night at the bar near the hotel in Australia. "Where did you get this?" he asked.

Ignoring the question, Mathieu asked, "What is going on here?"

Now Tristan understood why Juliette had been so curt. "I got in late to Sydney. All I wanted to do was head to the hotel and sleep because of the trip and the change in time. My friend

Jackson sent a car to pick me up. But when I got in, a real estate broker, who is Jackson's fiancee's boss, asked if I'd go get a drink with him.

"I don't drink and told the guy so, but he insisted. I figured I'd be there less than an hour and then get some sleep for the night."

"Is there a point to this backstory? Because I'm bored already." Mathieu looked at him with a raised brow.

Irritation rippled through Tristan. "Yes. Once we got there, I ordered my soda while the other guy drank and talked to some girls who approached us. One of them came up and kissed me. I pulled away as fast as I could and walked out of the room. I promise."

"So, you don't have any other girlfriends or flings going on at the same time you're dating our sister?" Henri's eyes narrowed, and even though he was a few inches shorter, he looked like he had the brawn to hold his own in a fist fight.

Running a hand through his hair, Tristan sighed. "No. I wouldn't do that to Juliette."

Henri looked at him, his expression vacant. "She told me about the fake relationship."

Tristan blinked several times, surprised at what he was hearing. For some reason, it hurt that she'd confessed to her brother about it. It was a ridiculous thought since the whole scheme was hers to begin with.

"I don't know how to show you that my feelings for her aren't fake. I came to Dinan in the hopes of getting the marketing contract for her company, but I don't really care about that anymore." The words caused him to open his eyes wide. It had been a long time since he'd wanted something that didn't relate to work or could impact his company.

"Go rest up. You'll be competing again in about an hour," Mathieu said.

The two men turned and moved away, causing a knot to form in Tristan's stomach. "So, what do I do about Juliette?"

Henri turned around and said, "Win the jousting competition, and then we'll talk."

"Does she even feel the same about me?" he called out, causing several people to turn and give him a curious look.

"Worry about that later," Mathieu called out as they walked away.

Tristan rubbed the back of his neck, frustrated with how things were going. He'd come here thinking he'd get the chance to solidify a real relationship with the artist and skin care owner, but all he'd gotten were a few more bruises. And if he had to joust over and over again, things were going to be rougher than surfing.

CHAPTER 31

*J*uliette worked to smile at the customers, filling orders and taking their money as she handed bags filled with different dishes and jewelry over the table time and time again. She wished her mind wasn't on the handsome man who'd come back looking so earnest in his excitement to see her.

Soon enough, her mother came to switch her out, giving her some much-needed time away from the booth. "Go find Tristan. I think your brother picked him up this morning. You look like you could use a little one-on-one time with him."

Pasting on a smile and moving away, she did her best to hide the tears and ducked into one of the doorways of the buildings closest to her. After all these years and the change of her face, she still couldn't believe someone would like her for her. Her instincts had been right. From the pictures Henri had shown her, it was obvious Tristan was all about kissing wherever and whoever came around.

She was done wasting her time pining for him. Besides, he'd only treated her as nice as he had because he wanted that contract. As much as she didn't want to, she knew she'd have to give it to him. The thought bored a hole in her heart that she didn't know how to heal. How could she have thought he'd have feelings for her when all he cared about was growing his company? He was using her to break into the beauty industry, and there was no way she could stand around and let him do that to her.

Moving out of the alcove, she pulled out her phone, dialing Rachelle. She turned in the direction of her parents' home, the tears falling freely.

"Hey, Juliette! How's the festival?" Rachelle asked in a bright voice. She must have heard a sob, because her tone changed, sounding soft. "What's wrong, girl?"

"I think I love him. And all he wants is that contract. How did I ever think I had a chance when he's been able to date all of the models of the world?"

Rachelle sighed. "Oh, Jules. I'm so sorry. What are you going to do? Did he fly back from Australia?"

She nodded even though Rachelle couldn't see it. "Yes, my brother picked him up this morning."

"Did you ask him outright how he feels for you?" Rachelle's tone was turning motherly, and Juliette wasn't in the mood for it.

"No. He'd probably look at me like I was crazy. He didn't sign up to date the ugly duckling."

With firm tone, Rachelle said, "You are no longer the ugly duckling. You started the relationship. End it on your terms."

After a brief pause, Juliette said, "There is a picture of him kissing another girl in Australia. Henri showed it to me yesterday."

"What? From all you've told me, Tristan has been a gentleman, the kind of guy who would go out of his way to do something for you. Do you really think he'd do that to you?"

Sighing, Juliette said, "I'm not sure what I think anymore. It's not like our relationship was binding, but it still hurts, you know? I felt like there was something between us, but that was probably just me being naïve about relationships and looking for chemistry when there wasn't any."

"What are you going to do about your agreement with him?" Rachelle asked.

"I'm not taking away the contract after he completed what we agreed to. But I don't think I can stay here any longer. Any emergencies that need my help?" She could hear the hope in her tone as she trudged up the stairs to her room.

"For starters, it's Saturday, so no one is in the office. Things are still running just as smoothly as the last time I called you."

"I've got to go, Rachelle. I'll see you soon." Hanging up before her friend could object, Juliette pulled the suitcase out from under her bed and piled all of her clothes inside. Making sure she'd packed everything, she pulled her bag down the stairs and out the door, walking in the direction of the booth.

As she approached, she saw her mom's face beaming at a customer. Juliette was grateful for the time she'd had these past weeks to work at home again. But her life was in Paris, and all of the tougher memories were still tied to Dinan. She was destined to be alone, and her heart ached at the thought.

Her mother saw her, and her smile faltered a bit. "You're leaving? Before the end of the festival?"

"I have to, Maman. There's a problem at the office, and I'm the only one who can fix it. I'll come out again soon. I promise."

With a sad smile and a tear falling down her cheek, her mother held out her arms, pulling her in for a hug. "I'll miss you, my dear. You've grown up so much and are so strong. Just remember that." She pulled back and said, "What about Tristan? Is he leaving with you? I just saw him a few minutes ago, looking for you."

"I'll try and find him." Juliette looked into her mother's eyes and wanted to cry all over again. She leaned in and said, "Tell Papa goodbye for me, will you?"

"Your sister is on her way here now. You can't wait long enough to see her?"

She shook her head and kissed her mother's cheeks before turning away so she wouldn't see the tears threatening to spill down her face.

Moving away, she started walking to the train, knowing it wasn't worth it to try and drive through the mess of the festival. Each step seemed like a weight had been thrown around her ankles, but she moved on, knowing she couldn't face all of the problems behind her.

She'd always thought of herself as a strong woman, but in the face of heartbreak, she'd turned into a coward, unable to face the man she loved.

Traitorous heart.

She wasn't sure how she'd fallen for him, but it wasn't something big or overpowering. It was the hundred small smiles, the dozen or so winks, and the ability to open up about her past that had done it. Not that the few kisses they'd shared were a bad deal. She could still feel his lips on hers, could close her eyes and remember every heartbeat as he'd held her head in his hands.

Shaking her head, she knew she was only digging deeper into the pain. She'd have to throw herself into her work and pretend she never met Tristan Delacroix at all.

Juliette had turned off her phone once she got on the train and hadn't turned it back on until the day after, when she'd called Rachelle to meet up for lunch.

When Rachelle walked into the café, Juliette could see the pity in her eyes and wanted to hide, wishing she hadn't wanted company.

"What are you doing here? Shouldn't you be selling jewelry and pottery in Dinan?"

Shaking her head, Juliette said, "No, I made all of it. My family can take it from there." She played with the fork on the table, turning it over and over again.

"Have you talked to Tristan?"

Biting her upper lip, Juliette said, "No. He's sent a few text messages, but I haven't had the heart to read them."

"Is this really about the contract? Or are you afraid that he actually might like you and you're running away?" Rachelle gave her a stern look, and Juliette had to look away.

"There's a picture of him kissing some girl in Australia last week. Obviously, his lips are a hot commodity for any girl who comes around. Why would I be anything special?"

Rachelle's lips rolled in, and her brows furrowed. "I'm sorry, Juliette. But you have to know that you are special. Look at what you've accomplished in your life. You could have resented the fact that you didn't have perfect skin and begrudged it forever. But you figured it out, and you moved forward. That's what you'll do with this whole situation. You'll find a way to make it work for you and be better because of it. This isn't the end of your world or the end of your relationships. All of the good things in life usually come after moments when we aren't sure we can move forward."

Juliette closed her eyes, resting her head on the back of the booth. She wished it were that easy, or that she could at least have a crystal ball to see the future.

Rachelle's phone rang, and she looked at Juliette before turning the phone so she could read the screen. Tristan Delacroix. "He's called every thirty minutes in the past few hours. I haven't answered, but I think it's time I do."

Reaching out, Juliette said, "Don't. Please, just leave it for later."

"Hello, Tristan." Rachelle gave her a sad smile, and Juliette was tempted to stand and leave, not ready to deal. Her friend agreed to a few things before she said, "She's right here."

"Traitor," Juliette mouthed to her.

Rachelle put her hand over the speaker on her phone and whispered, "I'm doing this for your own good. If anything, you can get the real story and move on. Otherwise, you'll be wallowing for days or weeks and never know what really happened." Something he said must have caught her attention, because she went back to the call.

Grabbing her purse, Juliette walked out of the café and down the road, not sure on a direction. Soon enough, she was standing next to the Seine River, leaning over the railing. How had her life turned so upside down? If she'd known she'd be going through this rollercoaster of emotions, would she have asked him to be her fake boyfriend? The lectures would've been easier than telling her parents the truth about her relationship with Tristan, especially when he had moved on.

"I've been looking for you everywhere." Tristan's voice came from behind her, and she turned, wishing she could disappear at that moment. A shiner was forming under one eye, and his hair was standing on end like he'd been pulling on it. It was all out of character for his put-together persona. "Why did you leave without telling me?"

Throwing her hands in the air, Juliette said, "There are a lot of reasons, but…" She tried to find the words and found her mind blank.

Tristan stepped forward, pulling her hands into his and looked down at her, more nervous than she'd ever seen him.

She lowered her gaze to their hands, fighting a new round of tears as her thoughts again raced to what could have been.

Tristan cleared his throat. "I know this relationship was supposed to be fake, and that I was motivated by that contract at the beginning, but I don't want it anymore."

His words stopped her, and she looked up, confused. "What do you mean? I thought that was the key to opening up a whole new industry for your company."

He nodded. "It could be. But I don't want it if it means I can't have you in my life. I—I love you, Juliette."

Pulling her hands out of his, she frowned. "Is this some game? Because you can't just play with someone's heart and then break it without a thought."

She turned, walking a few steps away, when he said, "Rachelle said you'd try to run."

Juliette stopped in her tracks. As much as she wanted to bolt away, she knew Rachelle had been right. She needed to face him, face her feelings and move on.

"How can you say you love me when you kissed another girl?" She looked him in the eyes, willing her knees not to give out at the pleading she saw there.

"I never kissed her. She kissed me. I was getting a soda with some guy Jackson knows, and when two girls started talking to us, I ignored them. But the girl walked up and kissed me. I pushed her away, and the first thing I thought of was you." He stepped forward hesitantly, placing his hands on her arms, the touch gentle and sending tingles throughout her upper body.

Closing her eyes, she blew out a breath, saying the first thing that came to her mind. "How can I know you're not just trying to manipulate me?" She opened her eyes, brows drawn together.

His face fell, and Juliette felt bad. "I came here to tell you that I love you, for real. But if you don't have feelings for me, just tell me now. I don't think I can bear to have someone dismiss me completely again."

Staring into his eyes, she saw the real hurt. Softening her expression, she reached up and touched his face, brushing his cheek with her fingers. "I love you too. I just never thought someone like you could want someone like me."

From the grin on his face, she'd have thought she'd just given him the moon. "Of course I do. You are like a breath of fresh air. You're spunky and good. I love that we can talk about anything and everything. That you don't automatically accept what I say because I have several zeroes in my bank account. And I love the way it feels when I kiss you."

He bent down, brushing his lips against hers.

Juliette stood, frozen for several seconds, reveling in feeling every nerve in her lips on fire. Leaning into him, she deepened the kiss, wrapping her arms around his neck and pulling him in. When they'd kissed for several seconds, she pulled back and said, "I thought I told you not to fall in love with me." She tilted her head back, looking into his eyes.

"I guess my heart just didn't listen." He said, leaning in for another kiss.

She heard a giggle from behind him. Breaking away, she saw her little family standing there, all smiles. Her parents, brothers, Isabelle, her sisters-in-law, nephews, and nieces.

"What are you all doing here? Shouldn't you be at the festival?" she asked, looking for an explanation from anyone in the group.

"Coline Viceny took over the booth for us. She knew this was so important to you and to all of us." Her father grinned at her, leaning heavily on Mathieu. "Tristan here made a valiant effort in the jousting tournament but ended up on the ground twice in a row, coming in fourth place."

Her four-year-old niece smiled. "He loves you, Auntie. We came to help him."

The group chuckled, only confusing Juliette more.

Her mother stepped forward, reaching for Juliette's hands. "Tristan told us everything, my dear. I'm sorry you felt you had to fake a relationship to make us happy. But after all he's told us, know that he is sincere."

"I interrogated him a bit, and it turns out I like him," her father said, winking at her. "Especially since he took some hard knocks in the joust. I believe that was your brothers' doing." He turned to stare at Henri and Mathieu.

Henri grinned, saying, "That was just a stalling tactic. We knew we'd get in trouble if we beat him up for Jules, so the best way to do it was to have someone else do it for us. If he'd quit after the first round, we wouldn't have known if he was willing to fight for you, Jules. But after talking to him, he is the real deal, and we just wanted you to know that no matter what you've both been through, maybe you can mend it together."

Juliette turned to look at Tristan, whose smile was soft and tender. She thought back to his words from moments before and was surprised that he hadn't said anything about her appearance. He'd called her beautiful before, but he liked her for more than what he saw on her face. "You really do love me?"

Tristan chuckled. "Yes, more than I thought possible from where we started." He kissed her again. "What do you say? Will you be my real girlfriend?"

Biting her bottom lip, she paused, looking up at him.

He gave her a worried expression before she said, "Yes, I'd love to be your real girlfriend."

With that, Tristan dipped her, staring into her eyes for a second before moving forward and kissing her. When he pulled her back up to a crowd of cheers, he leaned forward and said, "Here's to a life that's never dull."

EPILOGUE

*J*uliette and Tristan had been dating for several months, and she was excited to finally be going on another trip together. With their schedules only getting busier as their businesses grew, it had been hard to break away for longer than a weekend trip to Dinan. She'd met Tristan's parents the month before when they'd returned from their travels to the States, and it had been a lot of fun to get to know them. Tristan's dad reminded her of an older version of Tristan, but his sense of humor was what made it fun to visit with them.

They'd flown to Australia twice spend more time with Jackson and Hailey. They'd visited in September for Jackson's wedding, and the beginning of November had been the perfect time for another trip before the holiday sales began. There hadn't been much time to get to know them the first trip because of the number of people who'd attended the wedding, but by the end of the second trip, she saw how well they fit together.

After a few days of surfing, during which Tristan had decided to sit on the beach and wait, they'd enjoyed their time touring Sydney with Hailey as the tour guide. Juliette was amazed that a woman who'd moved there only a few months before could know so much about the city. But with the number of homes around the area that Hailey represented as a real estate agent, Juliette understood how she could become familiar with it so fast.

Tristan drove her into the heart of Sydney, and as they walked around the Royal Botanic Gardens, Juliette was amazed at the beauty of it all, right next to Sydney Harbor.

Taking her hand, Tristan said, "I want to show you something." They walked along the water, and she admired the colorful sky as the sun began to set, the Sydney Opera House in front of them. The rays of purple, red, orange, and yellow made her sigh, not wanting this week to end.

"This is perfect. We need to get away more often."

The corners of Tristan's mouth turned up. "Which means we both need to hire more people to cover for us while we're gone."

Laughing, Juliette said, "Agreed. I could use a few more people out in production. And bumping Rachelle up to manager would make her happy."

"Angela has been waiting for me to say I need to hire another manager. Apparently, our contract with some skin care company is causing us to have more work come in than we've had in years." He turned, sliding his hands around her waist and pulling her closer.

They kissed, several soft pecks, before Tristan took a step back. There was a moment of panic in his eyes that struck panic in her in return.

"Are you all right? What's wrong?"

He chuckled, the sound coming from deep down. "Nothing. I just wanted to say that the last few months with you have been eye-opening for me. I worried for years that the closer I got to a woman, the faster she'd run, just like Camila had. But being with you seems to have completely healed those wounds, and I'm forever grateful for it."

He blew out a breath, and Juliette hoped he wasn't having some sort of attack. She'd never seen him so out of sorts, and it kind of unnerved her.

"I feel the same. I always thought that every man only saw the outside appearance, but you proved that theory wrong, and I love you for it."

When he knelt down, she gasped, not sure if she was awake or just dreaming.

"Juliette Mathilde Rousseau, I've already asked your father for his permission, but I want to ask you the question I've been thinking about since that day by the Seine. Will you marry me?"

He pulled out a box from his pocket and opened it, holding it out for her.

Tears clouded her vision, and she couldn't even see what it looked like as she gazed down at the man she loved.

"I can't wait to spend the rest of forever with you." She pulled him up and kissed him. The sensation was full of excitement and, now, hope for the future. Wrapping her arms around his neck, she parted her lips, allowing him to deepen the kiss.

After a few seconds, he pulled back and asked, "So, is that a yes?"

Juliette laughed and nodded. "That's a yes."

He spun her around, her legs flying out as they turned. When he came to a stop, he leaned forward and kissed her lightly. "I love you, my cygne."

CHAPTER 1

THE BRITISH BILLIONAIRE

*P*acing back and forth behind the bus stop enclosure, Isabelle Rousseau dialed her sister, Juliette. It had been one of those awful weeks where even with her best efforts, she'd failed. The stifling mid-July air of the London afternoon didn't help her spirits either.

Her sister answered after the second ring. "Hey, sis. How are you?" Isabelle could hear the papers shuffling in the background, meaning Juliette was still at work.

Pulling the phone back to look at the time, Isabelle realized it was only two in the afternoon. She'd put off this call long enough, and she hoped her sister could at least hear her out before offering some perfect answer Isabelle should have been thinking about before.

"Do you have a minute?" she tried to say as calmly as possible, fighting to keep the tears at bay and her voice stronger than she felt. Juliette was dedicated to the skin care company she'd started a few years before, and even though she was only two years older, some-times Isabelle felt like it was more like five. At twenty-five, Isabelle hadn't quite "made it", still working as an assistant to an interior designer. As happy as she was for Juliette's success, there were still times a shot of envy reared its head.

"Rough day with Darcy?" Juliette paused, and Isabelle kept silent, not ready to say anything about her boss, knowing it would only add ammo to the fire. "I don't know why you continue to work for her."

Twisting a lock of her dark brown hair around one finger, Isabelle stared at the ground as she paced, her annoyance easing somewhat as she had someone to vent to.

"I know. You say this every time I have a rough day, but I need this job. Darcy Stewart is the best interior designer and stager in London. With her approval, I can get any job I want just from sticking it out." Isabelle sucked in a breath, waiting for her sister's response.

"But for how long, Isa? If you don't stand up to her now, how are you going to do it five years down the road when you have another job offer? I think you're too comfortable."

"Too comfortable?" she shouted and paused as several heads snapped in her direction. With the adrenaline pumping through her now, she lowered her voice and said, "There is no way I'm too comfortable. I think she's giving me an ulcer."

Juliette chuckled. "You always were a little dramatic. Maybe you should take a vacation. You haven't had one of those in the three years you've worked for her."

Isabelle frowned and stopped walking. A vacation sounded wonderful. But she knew it would only end in having to field Darcy's phone calls at all hours.

"I just wish there was a way to be a stager for myself. Everyone around here needs a million recommendations, but I don't have a name established within the industry."

"That isn't the worst thing in the world. You've got some savings. Do the math. How long can you go without a paycheck to tide you over? Do as much as you can to prepare for your business, make a business plan, and then give your notice. I can have Tristan help you with a marketing plan." Isabelle could picture her sister's face, matter-of-fact and no-nonsense.

As much as she appreciated the help, she wasn't sure she wanted her sister's fiancé to help her. He was a nice enough guy, but she couldn't help but feel intimidated when he was around. Although, she'd only met him once when she'd gone back home at the beginning of the month. Tristan had come with Juliette that weekend to set up something else for her parents' business. They were the perfect match, billionaire marketing exec and self-starter skin care guru.

Isabelle rolled her eyes. Things like the perfect man coming into her life didn't happen to Isabelle.

"I didn't call to talk about work or what my five-year plan should look like." Isabelle closed her eyes, leaning against the building nearest the stop. Putting a hand on her forehead, she said, "Aaron broke up with me. Two nights ago."

Silence permeated through the phone, and Juliette's voice was softer when she spoke. "I'm so sorry, Isabelle. Did he give you a reason why?"

A tear rolled down her cheek, and she took a few extra seconds to compose herself. "I'm not good enough for him."

"Please tell me he didn't say that. If he did, he's more of an idiot than I expected."

Isabelle's jaw dropped. "What do you mean, 'idiot'? You just met him three weeks ago, and you said he was nice."

"Nice? You thought that's what I'd say to give my approval for your fiancé?" Juliette's words called up a familiar image in Isabelle's head, the look Juliette had perfected over the course of her lifetime. Her eyes took on a bored expression while she pursed her lips, looking displeased.

Shaking her head, Isabelle said, "Why didn't you come out and say it, then? It would have saved me time." She was near shouting now and turned to face away from the other people waiting in the area.

"Would you have listened? You looked pretty smitten to me."

"Probably not."

Juliette sniffed. "Tell me what happened."

Isabelle thought about the night she'd gone out with Aaron, how excited she'd been to try the new restaurant that had opened in London. He was from a very well-to-do family, and there had been several perks over the course of their six-month relationship. But she should have listened to her gut after meeting his parents two weeks before. Things hadn't gone well, and her more humble upbringing was called into question.

"He picked me up, and instead of going to dinner like we'd planned, the driver drove down a few streets and stopped. Aaron turned to me and said, 'This isn't going to work out. If I'm going to make it to Parliament, I need someone who understands business just as much as I do. You're beautiful, but all this design stuff will get you nowhere.'"

"Do you believe him?"

The question stunned Isabelle, and she didn't move for a moment, reconsidering her words.

"Yes."

"About which part?" Why did Juliette have to be so annoying when she was right?

"About all of it. His parents looked at me like the gum stuck to the bottom of their shoes. I wasn't after their money. I just thought I loved their son. Turns out he didn't feel the same."

She wiped at the tears flowing freely now. Taking a sip from the cup of tea she held, she turned to look for the bus. When her sister didn't say anything, she said, "And I really don't know much about business anyway."

"You can, though. You've got the head for it. And the parts you don't know or don't want to deal with, you hire out. Isabelle, I'm serious. You have a great eye for design. I come into my office every day since you've decorated it and have to smile because it's amazing and it reminds me of you."

Isabelle had come up short several times in her life, but nothing showed it more than comparing herself to her sister. Juliette had to overcome so much with her skin problems as a teen and had made something good of it.

Was that the trick? Isabelle would have to endure some great tragedy to be blessed as well as her sister?

"I don't know if I could start my own business, Jules. It just seems like a lot of work when all I want to do is design and stage."

"Think about it. I've got a lot of experience myself and would love to get my favorite sister out of the clutches of Darcy Stewart."

Isabelle laughed. "I'm your only sister." After a few moments, she said, "I'll think about it over the weekend and let you know."

"I have a meeting in about five minutes." Juliette paused. "I'm really sorry about Aaron, Isa. I know how much you wanted it to be him."

"Thanks, Jules. I'll let you go." She couldn't mask the resigned tone in her voice and took in a deep breath, feeling more alone than ever.

"You'll figure it out, sis." The line went dead, and Isabelle stared at her phone as if the answer to her problems was going to appear on the screen.

ACKNOWLEDGMENTS

Thank you so much for reading this book! I hope you enjoyed it and make sure to leave a review!

It's already been so much fun to research and learn more about the people of these different countries and I can't wait until I can visit all the countries.

I'd like to thank Sandra Paquet for helping me read through the rough draft to get all of the facts right. That's one of the things I love about being an author is the opportunity to work with so many amazing people who make my writing better and Sandra definitely did that for this book!

My husband deserves a lot of credit here as he takes care of life while I get these books ready to be published. Thank you, Max, for believing in me and for helping me realize my other dream.

Julie L. Spencer, Elizabeth McCay, Shannon Symonds and Deborah Goodman. Some of the best and funnest romance people I could associate with. I love our Thursday night chats and the late hours talking about whatever is going on in our lives. The long Facebook threads and the fun laughter as we work through our bad first drafts down to the final edits.

To Christina Schrunk for her patience in working with me on

these books. Her ideas and insight help to spark those last final puzzle pieces to help the book come together and I am so grateful for her.

To Krista Burdine for proofreading this book. She keeps me sane so I don't have to reread the book 100 times before publishing to hopefully get all of the errors out.

To Blue Valley Author Services, AKA Victorine Lieske and her awesome sister for making the cover. Especially for the last minute change of the guys eyes.

If you want news on when the next book comes out or my progress on the series, make sure to subscribe to the list so you don't miss anything.

I am grateful for readers like you and can't wait for you to enjoy the next book!

ABOUT THE AUTHOR

Britney Mills was born in Utah but parts of her heart lie in Boston, Washington D.C. and Germany. Her love of writing began with the third grade book her teacher assigned her to write and she spent hours hidden behind her mother's couch writing pages and pages about knights and castles. Now she writes about romance. Go figure.

When she's not mothering her four small children, writing or reading, she's probably out playing a sport, going on a hike, or binge watching a murder mystery series. The way to her heart is through homemade chocolate chip cookies and five minutes peace.

www.ingramcontent.com/pod-product-compliance
Lightning Source LLC
Chambersburg PA
CBHW030753200726
48288CB00004B/1159